FAR OUT
FAIRY TALES

INTRODUCING...

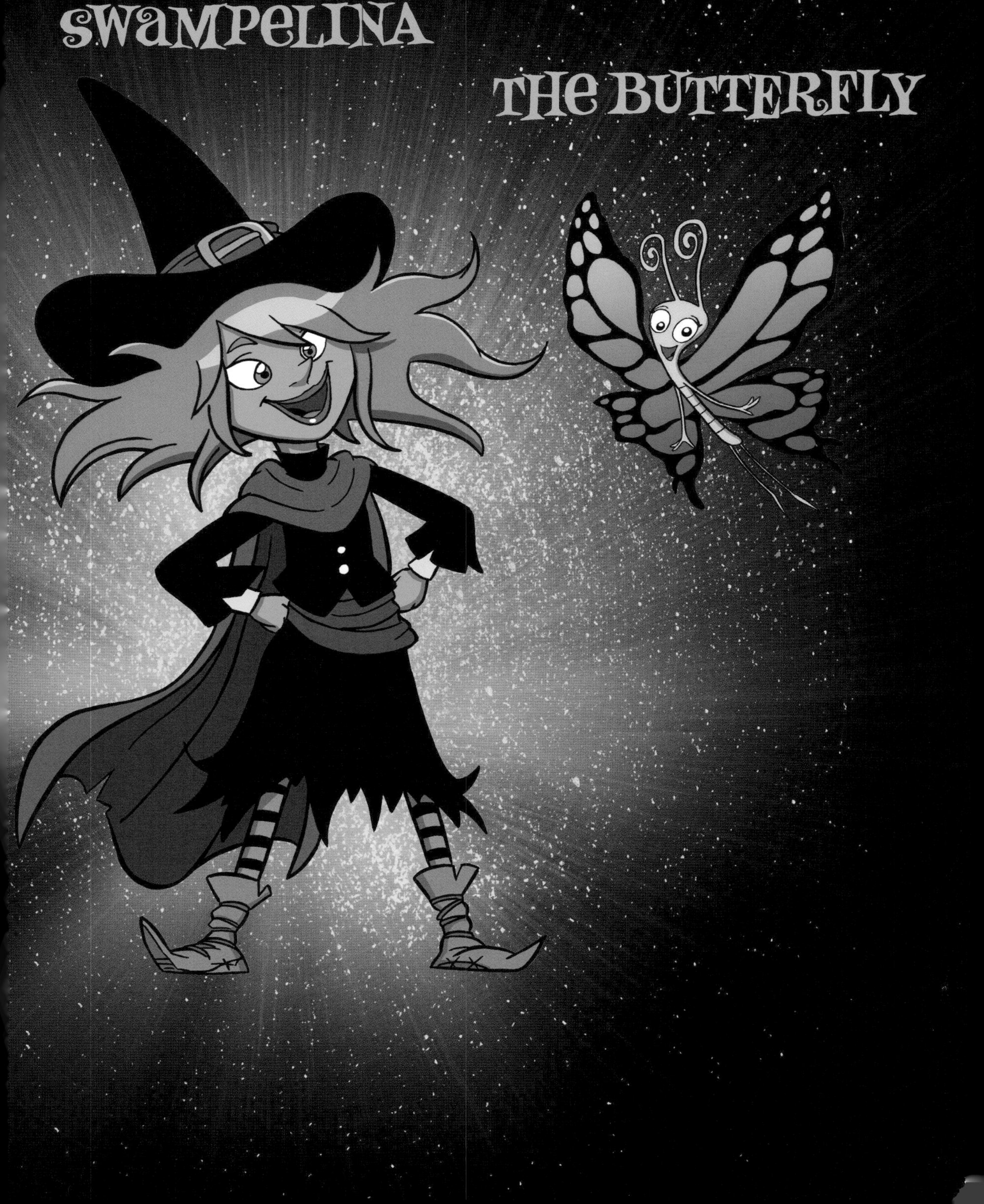
SWAMPELINA
THE BUTTERFLY

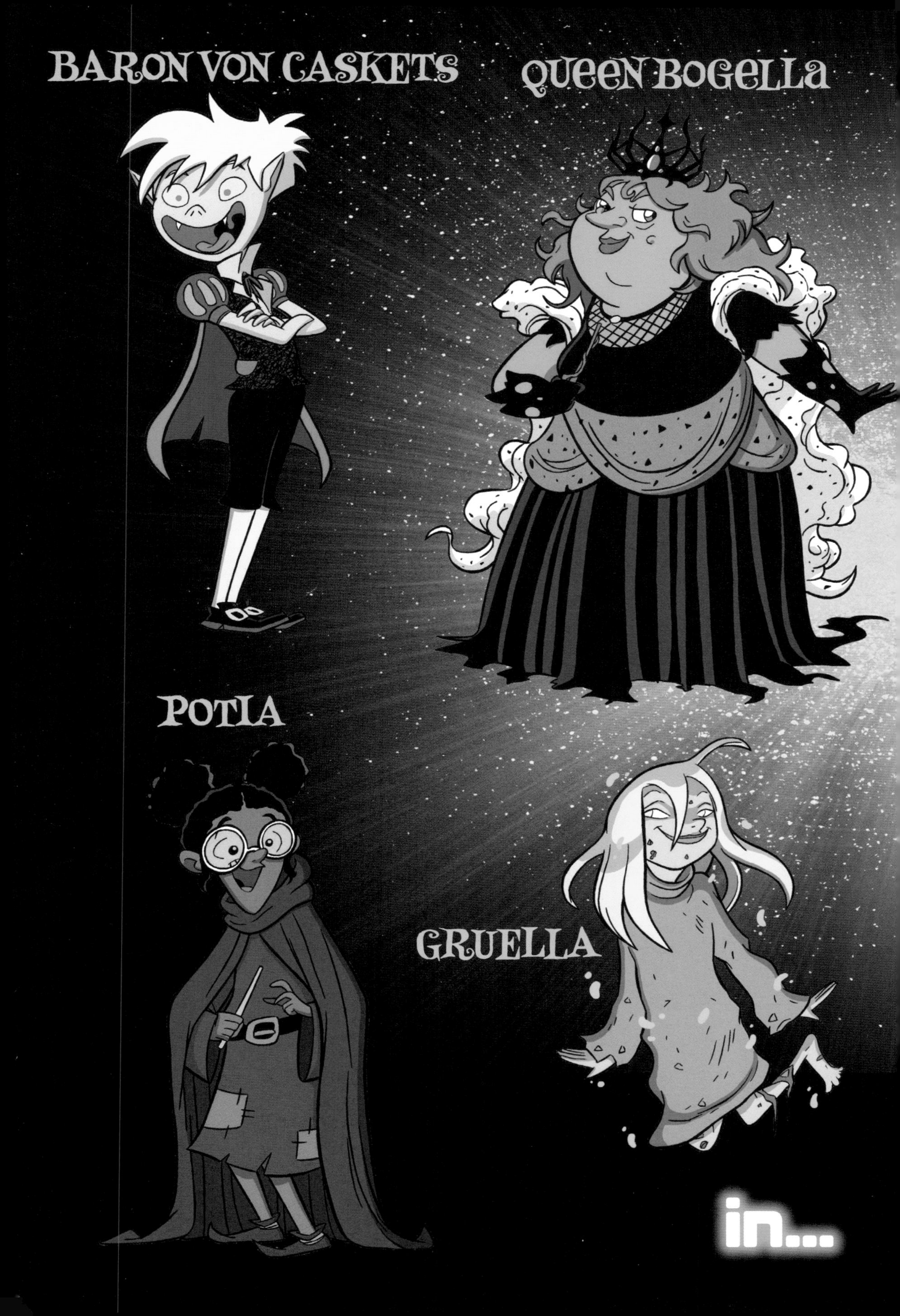
BARON VON CASKETS
QUEEN BOGELLA
POTIA
GRUELLA
in...

Published by Stone Arch Books,
an imprint of Capstone.
1710 Roe Crest Drive
North Mankato, Minnesota 56003
capstonepub.com

Library of Congress Cataloging-in-
Publication Data
Names: Harper, Benjamin, author. |
Lopez, Alex, 1976- illustrator.
Title: The frog prince's curse : a
graphic novel / by Benjamin Harper ;
illustrated by Alex López.
Other titles: Far out fairy tales.
Description: North Mankato,
Minnesota : Stone Arch Books, an
imprint of Capstone, 2022. | Series:
Far out fairy tales | Audience: Ages
8–11. | Audience: Grades 4–6. |
Summary: When the young witch
Princess Swampelina loses her wand in
the bog, a beautiful (ugh!) butterfly
offers to retrieve it if she will be his
friend, but after first avoiding him,
the princess soon finds the butterfly
helpful and even rather fun.
Identifiers: LCCN 2022004730
(print) | LCCN 2022004731 (ebook)
| ISBN 9781666335491 (hardcover)
| ISBN 9781666335446 (paperback)
| ISBN 9781666335415 (pdf) | ISBN
9781666335460 (kindle edition)
Subjects: LCSH: Frog Prince (Tale)–
Adaptations. | Butterflies–Comic
books, strips, etc. | Butterflies–
Juvenile fiction. | Princesses–Comic
books, strips, etc. | Princesses–
Juvenile fiction. | Blessing and
cursing–Comic books, strips, etc. |
Blessing and cursing–Juvenile fiction. |
Promises–Comic books, strips, etc. |
Promises–Juvenile fiction. | Fairy
tales. | Graphic novels. | CYAC:
Butterflies–Fiction. | Witches–Fiction.
| Blessing and cursing–Fiction. |
Promises–Fiction. | Fairy tales. |
Graphic novels. | LCGFT: Fairy tales.
| Graphic novels.
Classification: LCC PZ7.7.H366
Fr 2022 (print) | LCC PZ7.7.H366
(ebook) | DDC 741.5/973–dc23/
eng/20220208
LC record available at https://lccn.
loc.gov/2022004730
LC ebook record available at https://
lccn.loc.gov/2022004731

Designed by Hilary Wacholz
Edited by Abby Huff
Lettered by Jaymes Reed

Printed and bound in the USA. PO4882

FAR OUT FAIRY TALES

THE FROG PRINCE'S CURSE

A GRAPHIC NOVEL

BY BENJAMIN HARPER

ILLUSTRATED BY ÁLEX LÓPEZ

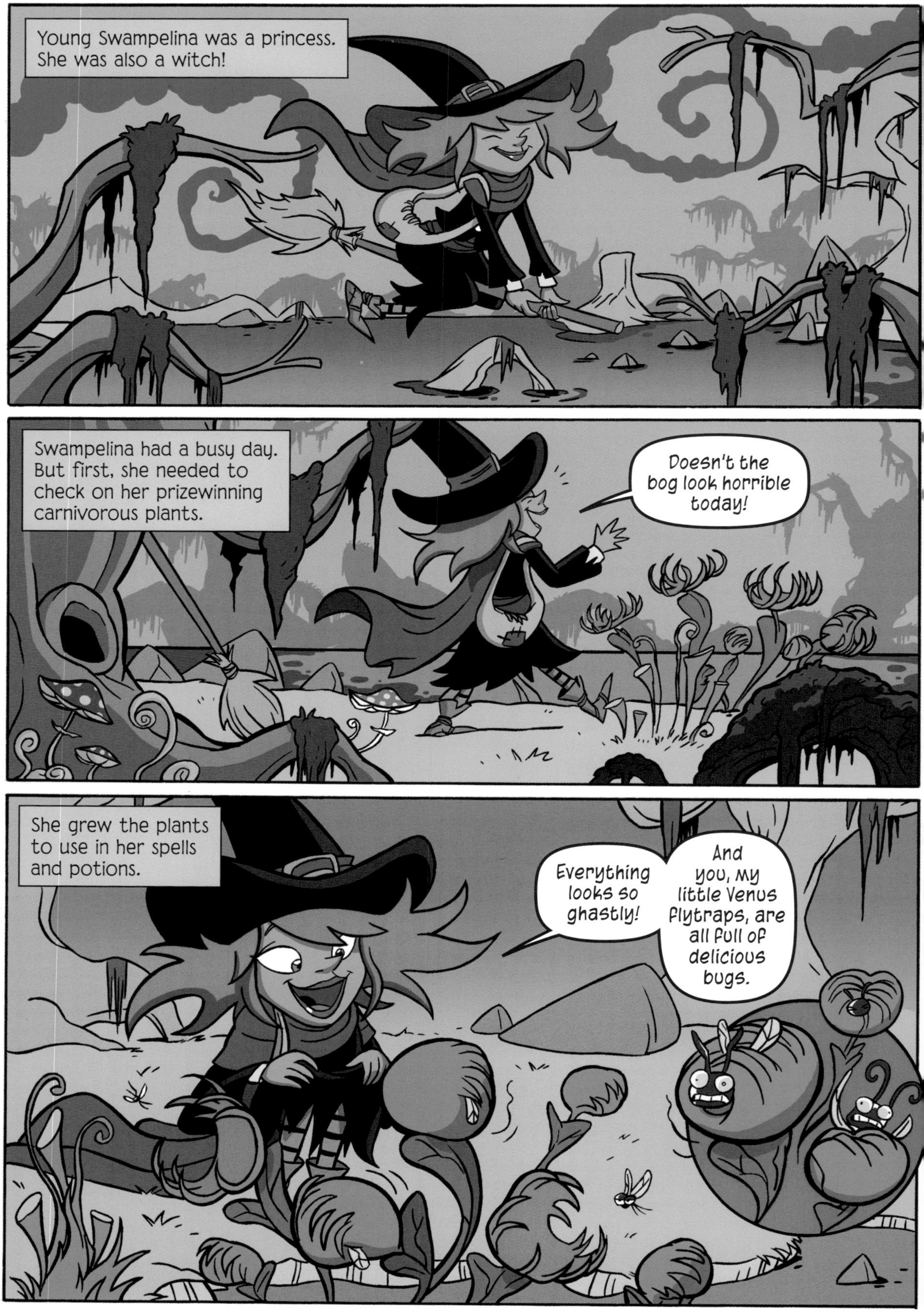

Young Swampelina was a princess. She was also a witch!
Swampelina had a busy day. But first, she needed to check on her prizewinning carnivorous plants.
Doesn't the bog look horrible today!
She grew the plants to use in her spells and potions.
Everything looks so ghastly!
And you, my little Venus flytraps, are all full of delicious bugs.

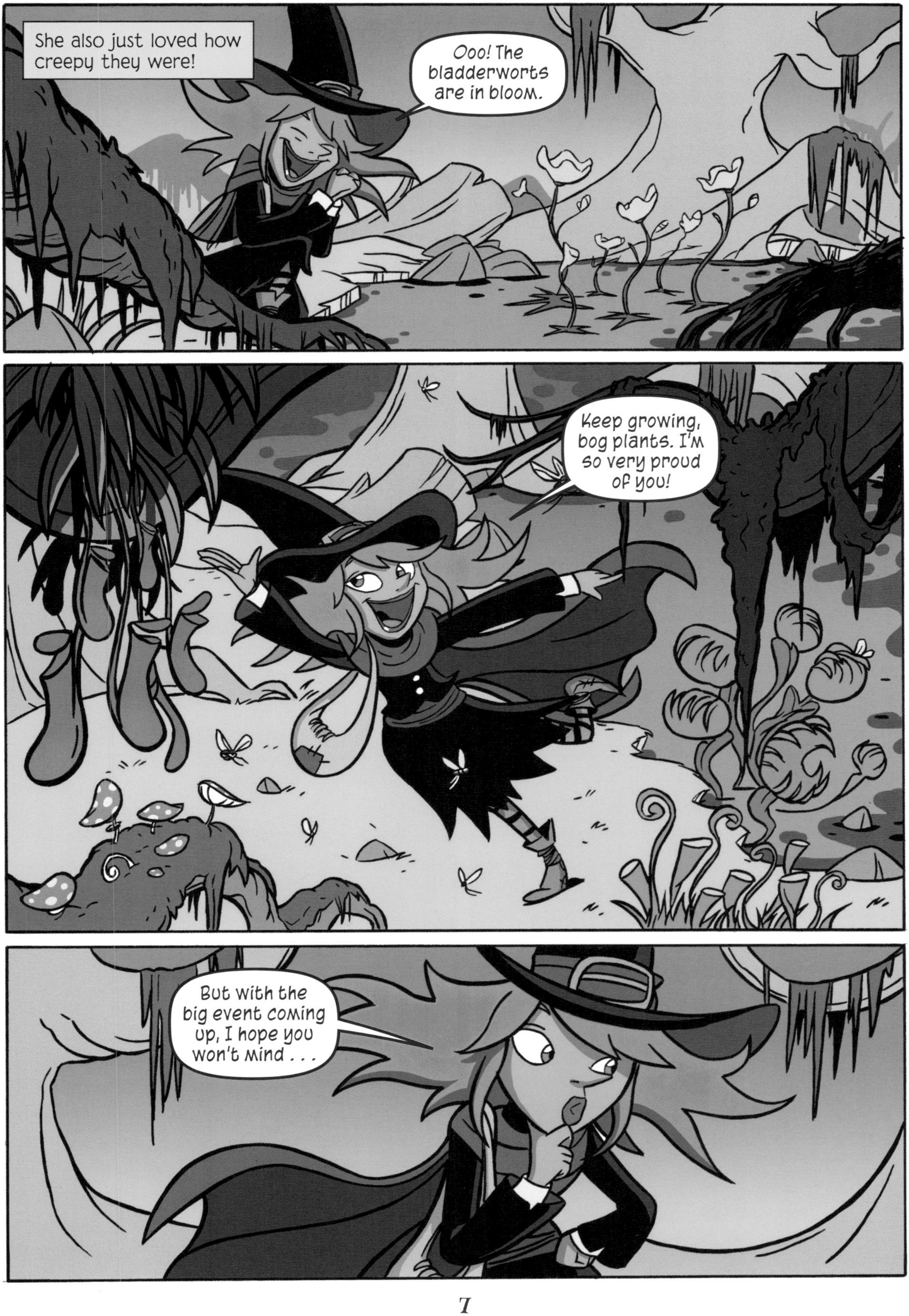
She also just loved how creepy they were!
Ooo! The bladderworts are in bloom.
Keep growing, bog plants. I'm so very proud of you!
But with the big event coming up, I hope you won't mind . . .

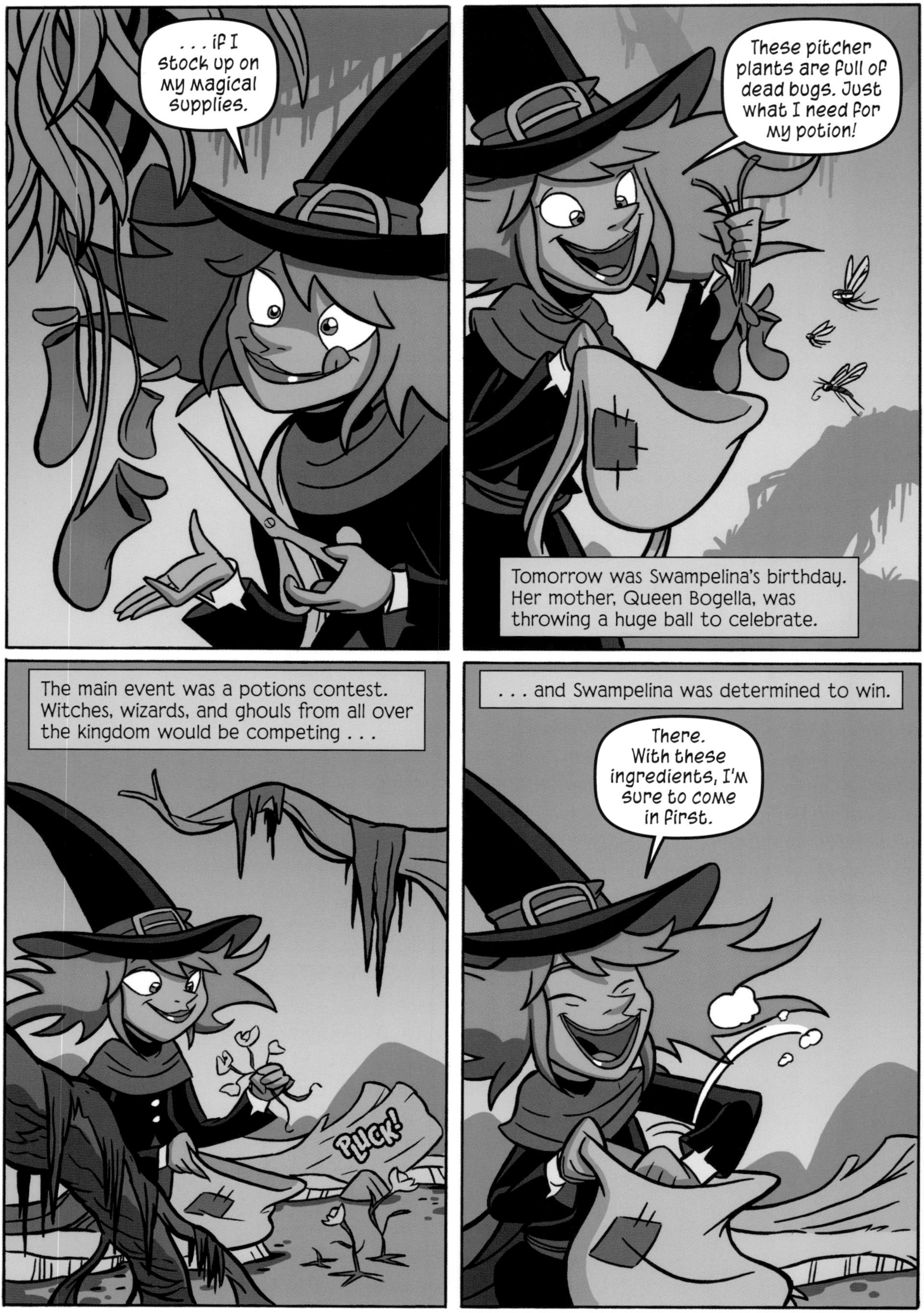
. . . if I stock up on my magical supplies.
These pitcher plants are full of dead bugs. Just what I need for my potion!
Tomorrow was Swampelina's birthday. Her mother, Queen Bogella, was throwing a huge ball to celebrate.
The main event was a potions contest. Witches, wizards, and ghouls from all over the kingdom would be competing . . .
PLUCK!
. . . and Swampelina was determined to win.
There. With these ingredients, I'm sure to come in first.

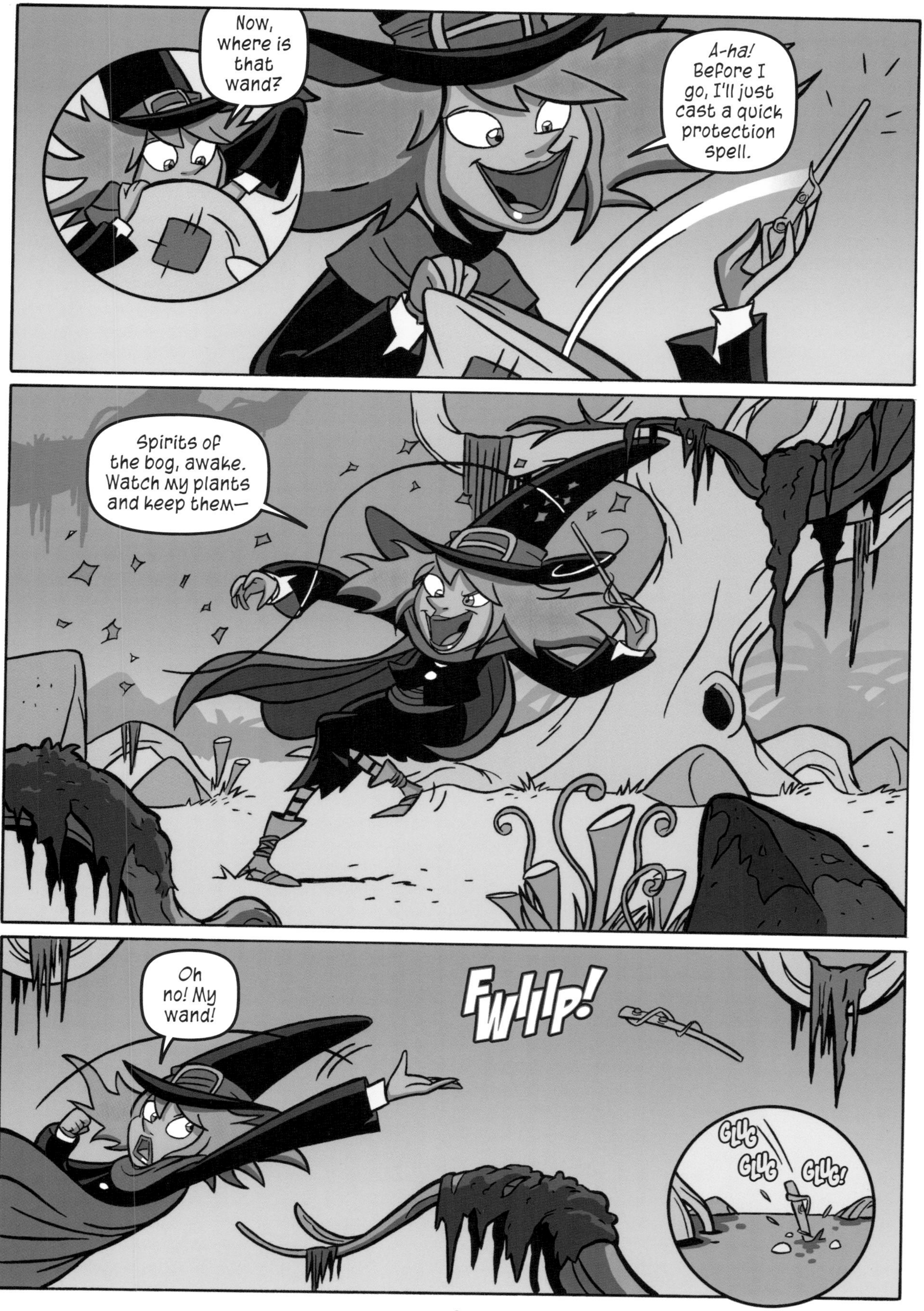
Now, where is that wand?
A-ha! Before I go, I'll just cast a quick protection spell.
Spirits of the bog, awake. Watch my plants and keep them—
Oh no! My wand!
FWIIIP!
GLUG
GLUG
GLUG!

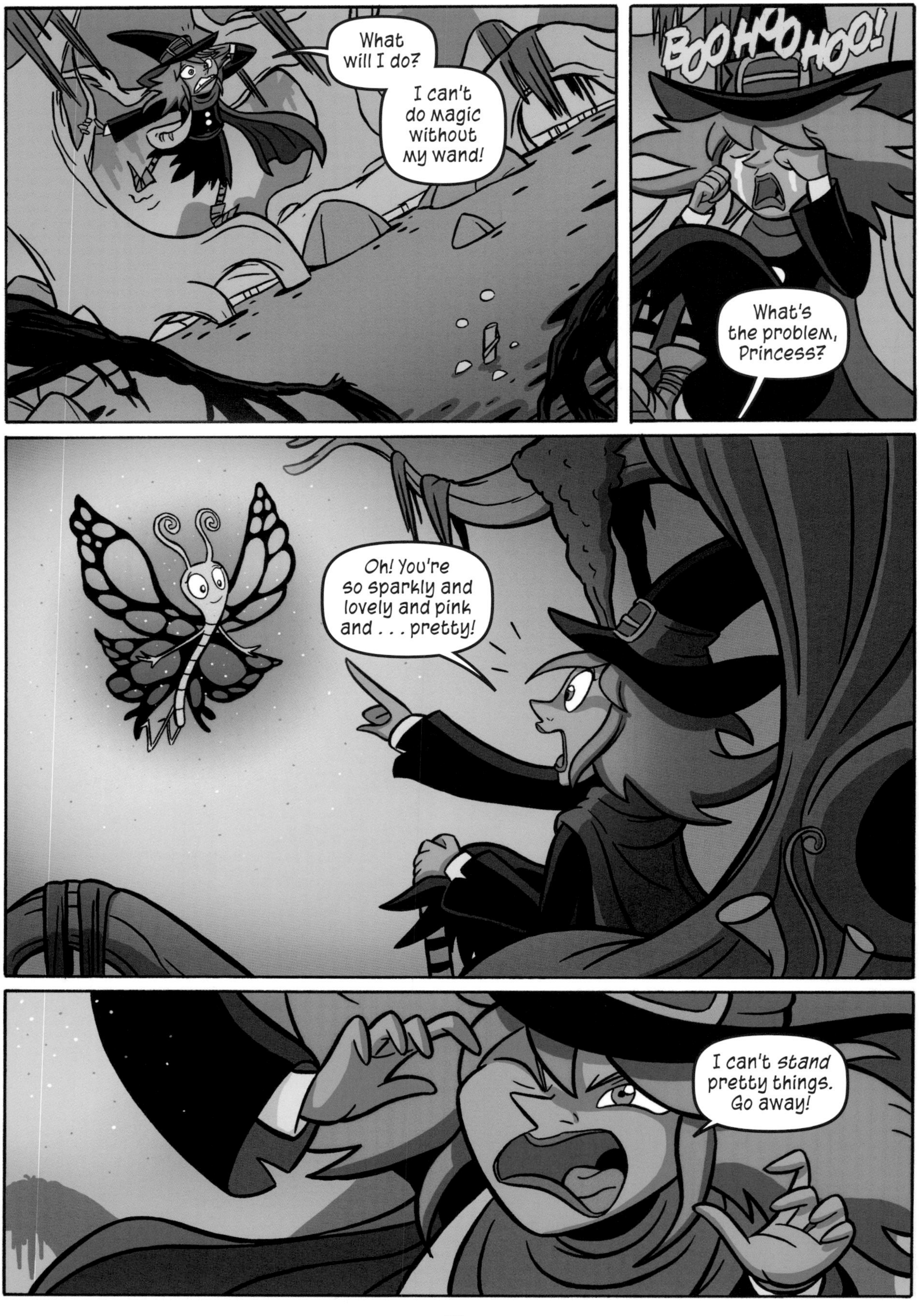
What will I do?
I can't do magic without my wand!
BOO HOO HOO!
What's the problem, Princess?
Oh! You're so sparkly and lovely and pink and . . . pretty!
I can't *stand* pretty things. Go away!

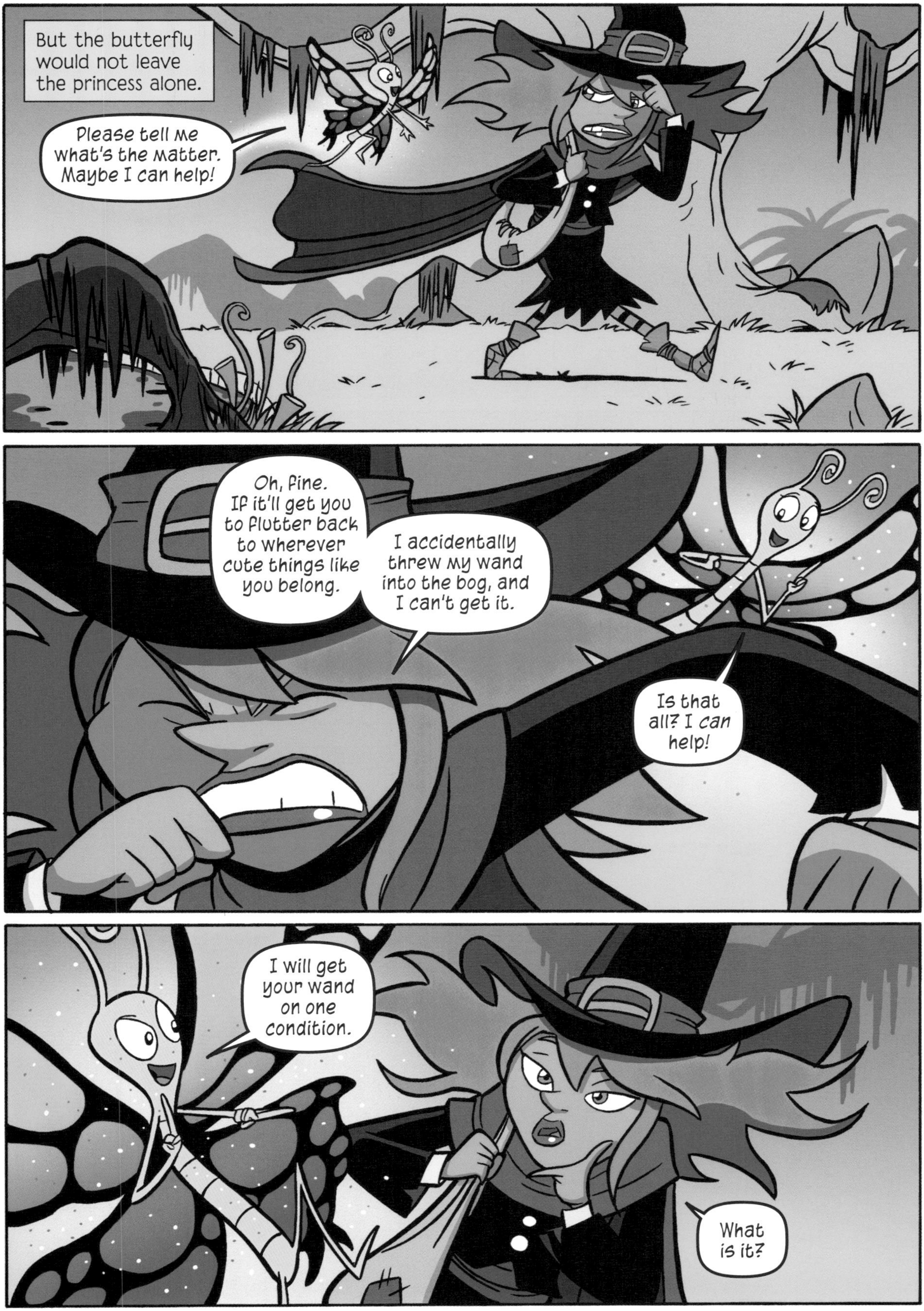
But the butterfly would not leave the princess alone.
Please tell me what's the matter. Maybe I can help!
Oh, fine. If it'll get you to flutter back to wherever cute things like you belong.
I accidentally threw my wand into the bog, and I can't get it.
Is that all? I can help!
I will get your wand on one condition.
What is it?

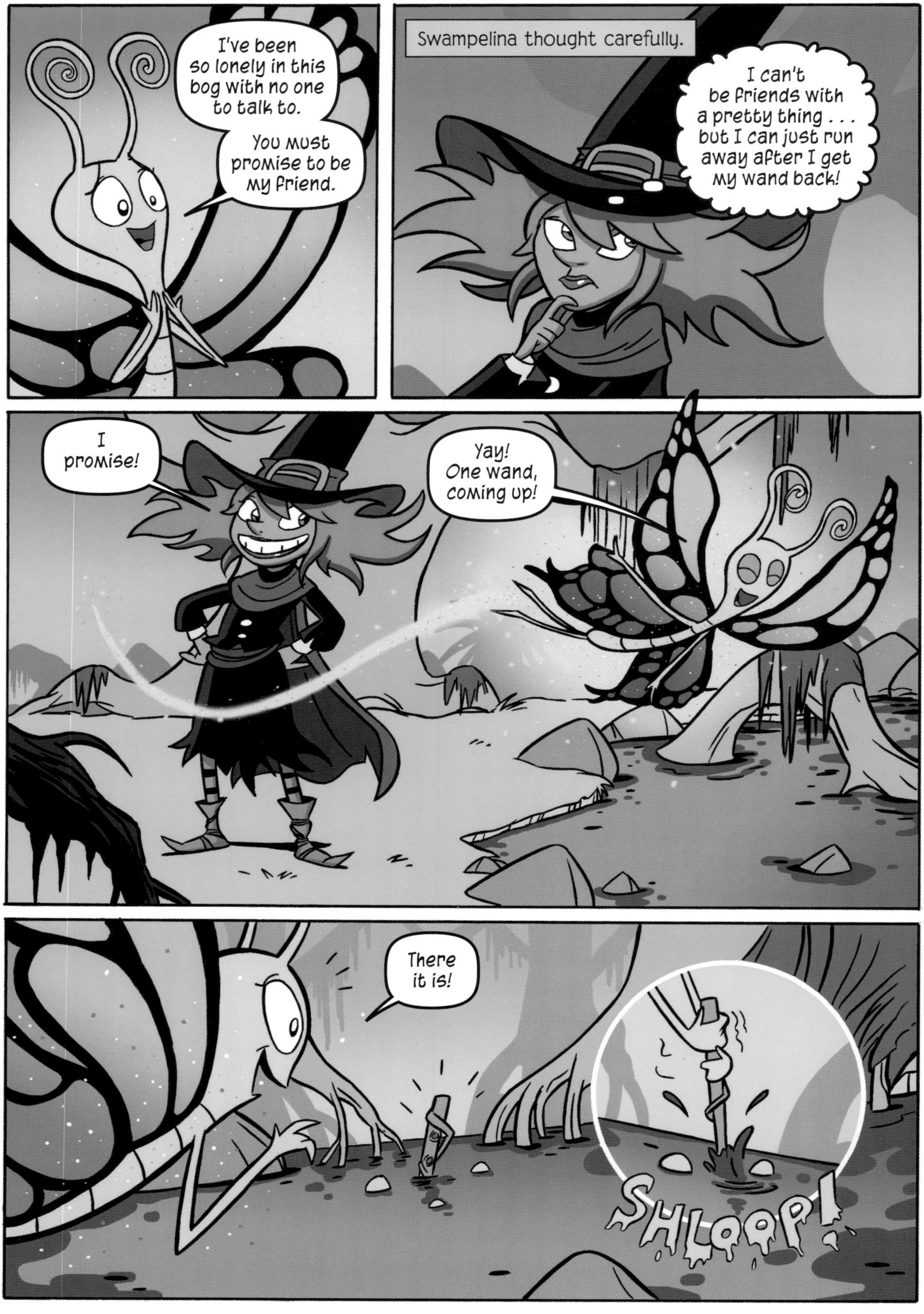
I've been so lonely in this bog with no one to talk to.
You must promise to be my friend.
Swampelina thought carefully.
I can't be friends with a pretty thing . . . but I can just run away after I get my wand back!
I promise!
Yay! One wand, coming up!
There it is!
SHLOOP!

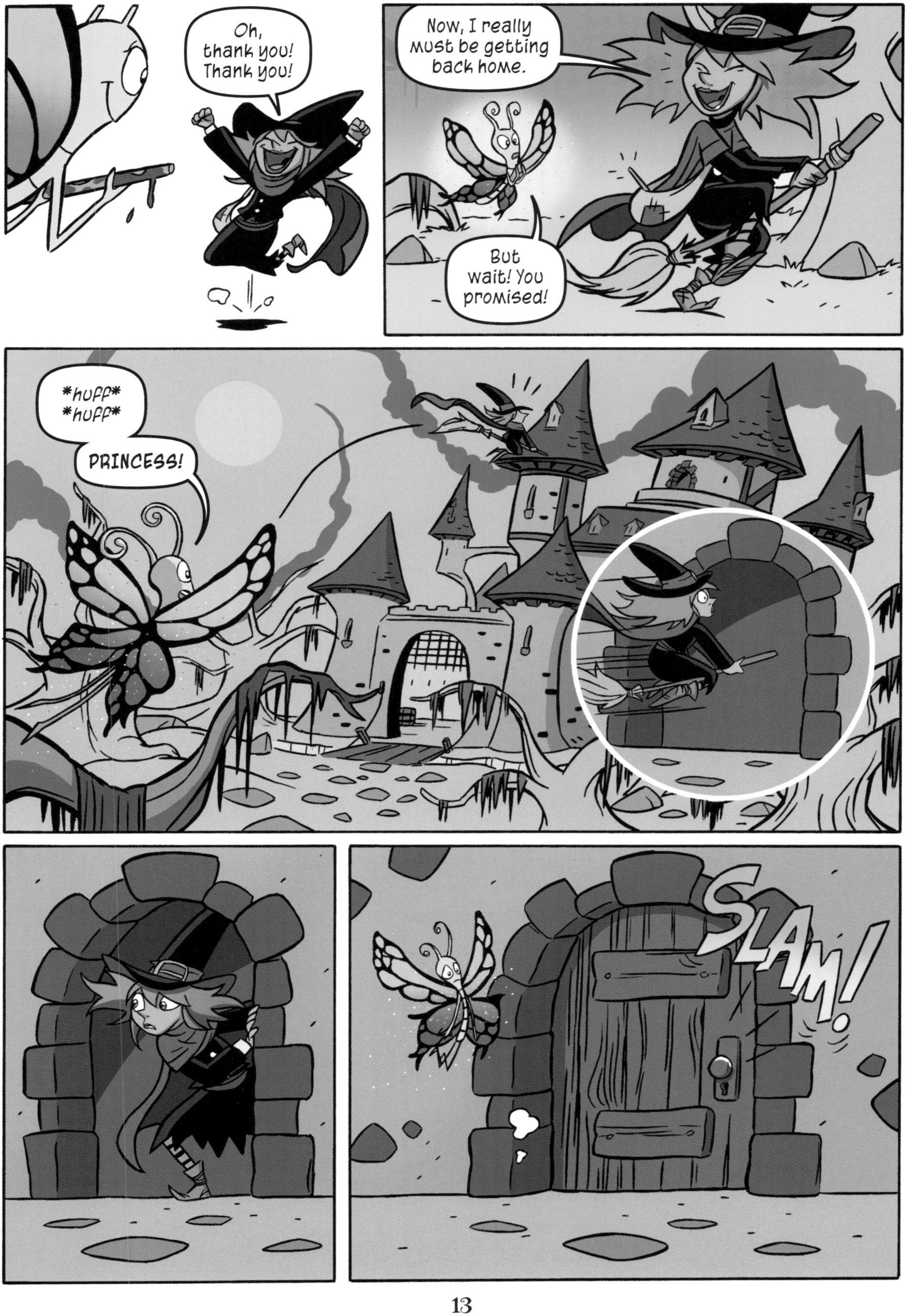
Oh, thank you! Thank you!
Now, I really must be getting back home.
But wait! You promised!
huff *huff*
PRINCESS!
SLAM!

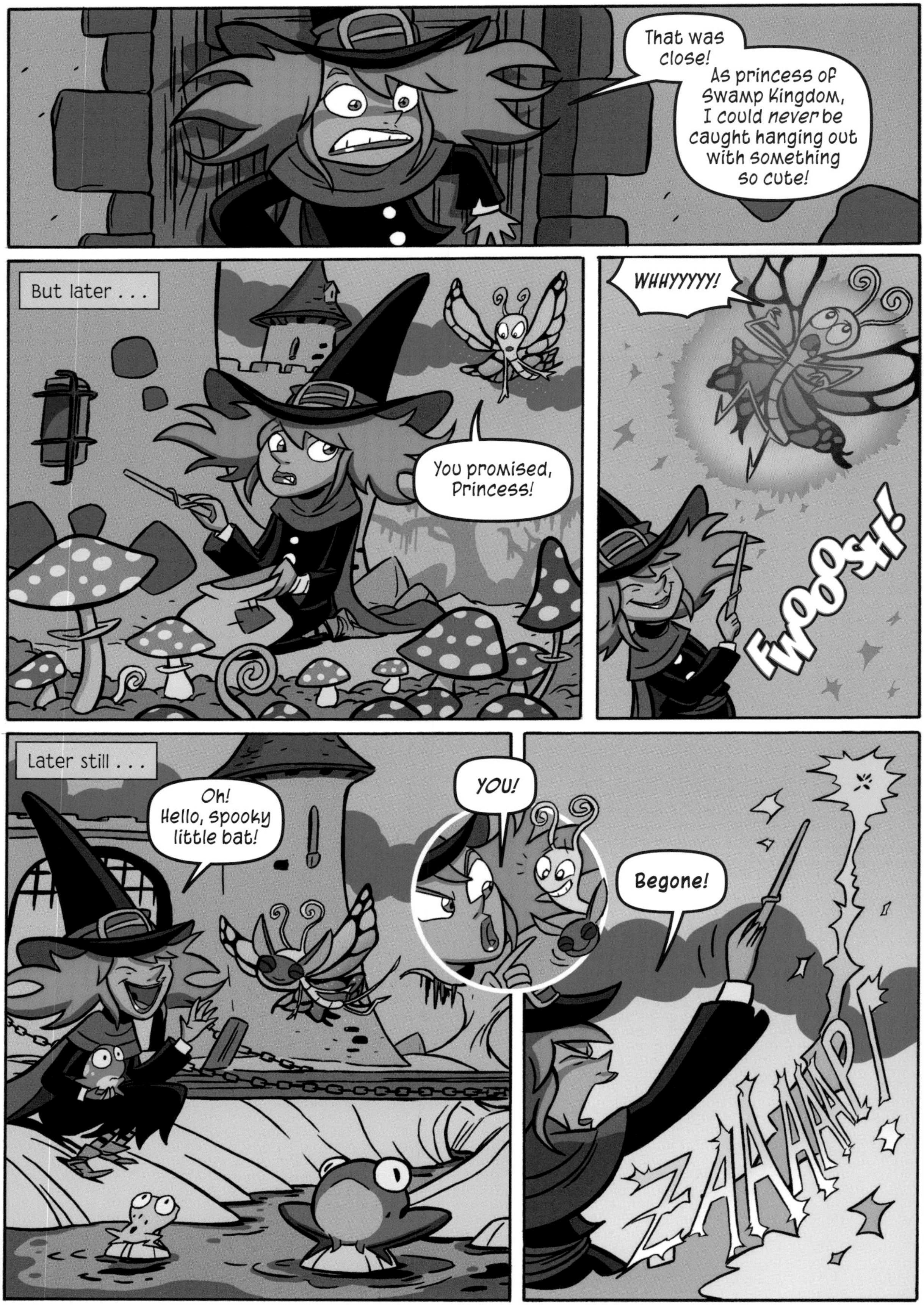
That was close!
As princess of Swamp Kingdom, I could *never* be caught hanging out with something so cute!
But later . . .
You promised, Princess!
WHHYYYYY!
FWOOOSH!
Later still . . .
Oh! Hello, spooky little bat!
YOU!
Begone!
ZAAAAP!

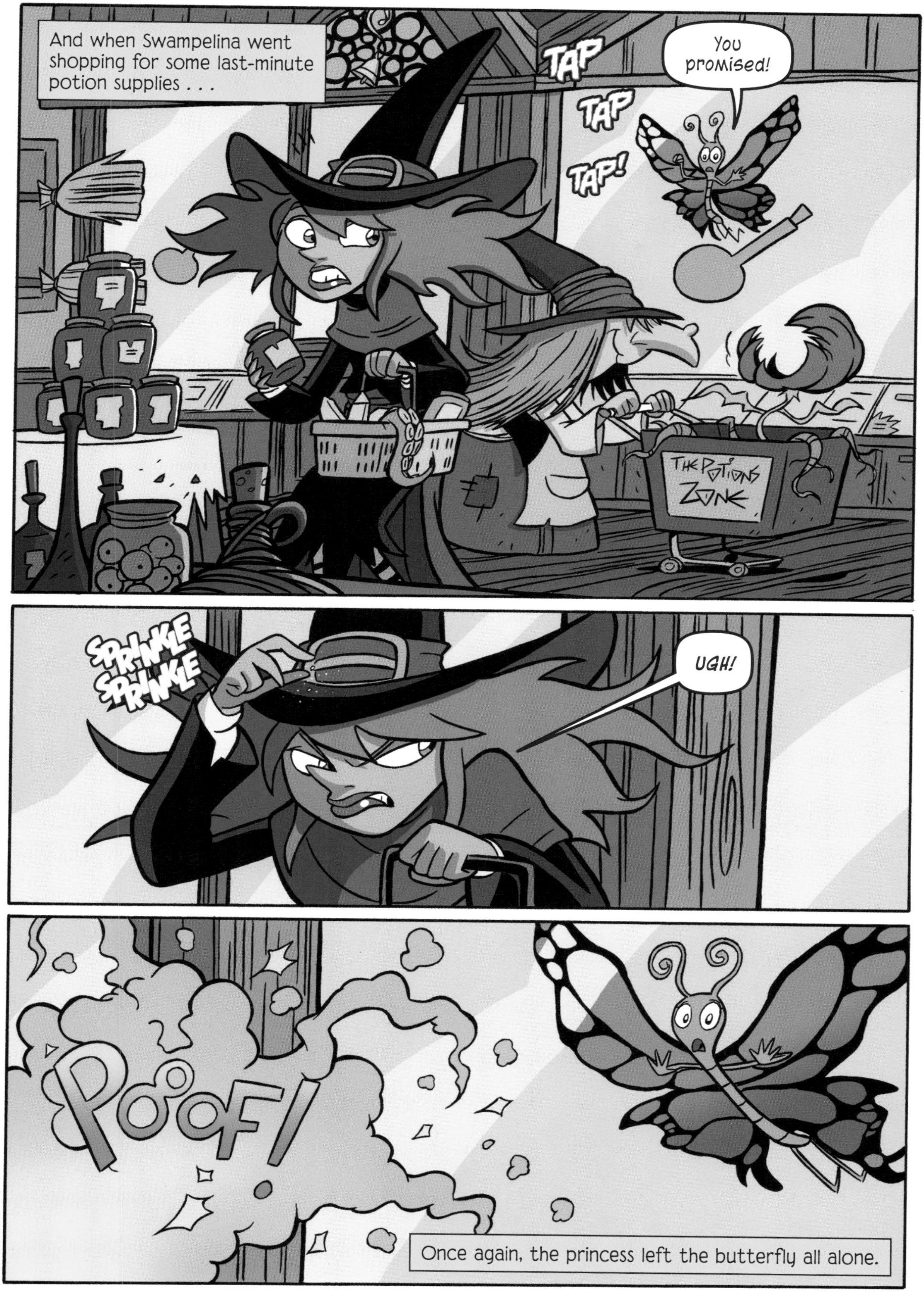
And when Swampelina went shopping for some last-minute potion supplies . . .
TAP
TAP
TAP!
You promised!
THE POTIONS ZONE
SPRINKLE SPRINKLE
UGH!
POOF!
Once again, the princess left the butterfly all alone.

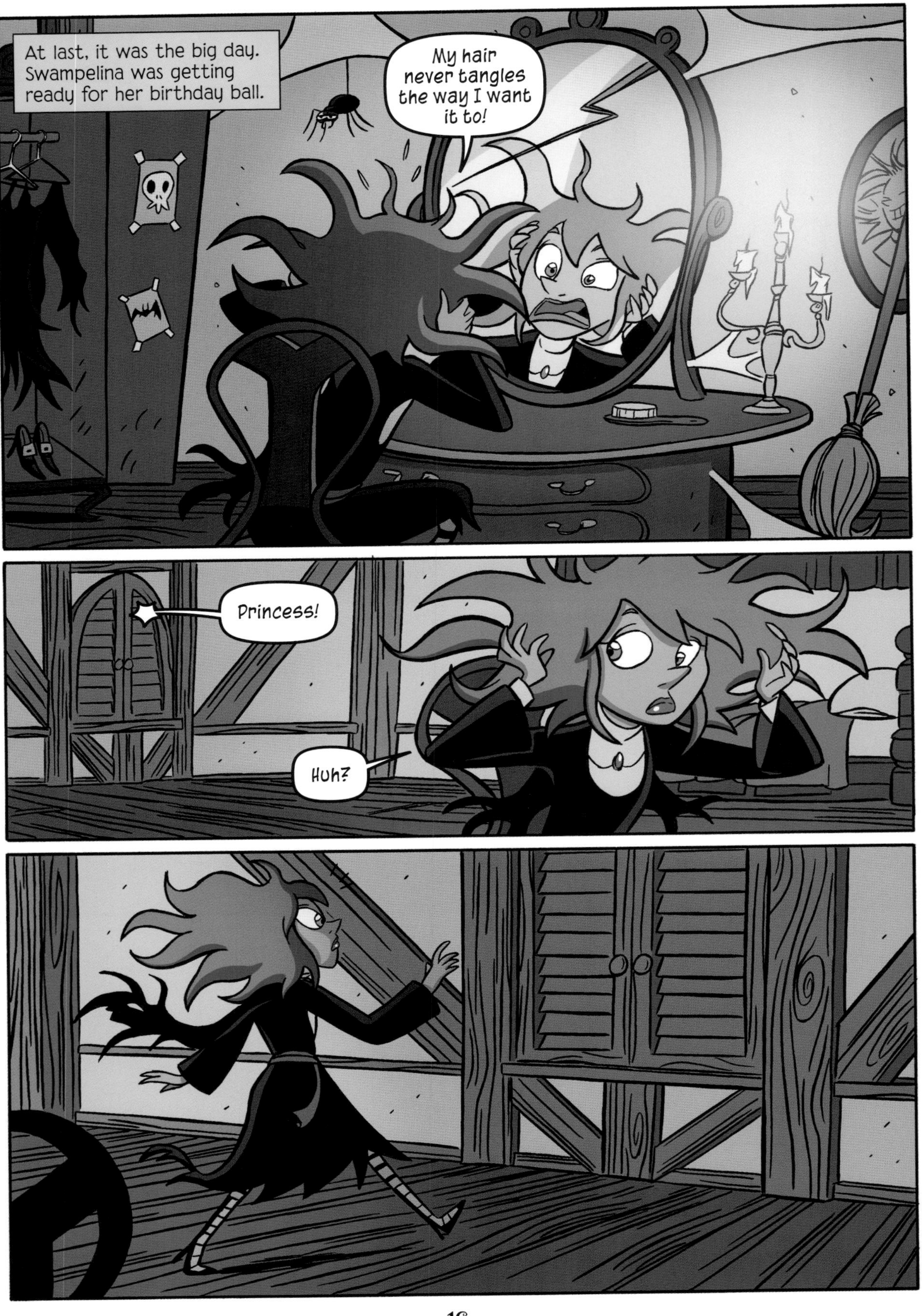
At last, it was the big day. Swampelina was getting ready for her birthday ball.
My hair never tangles the way I want it to!
Princess!
Huh?

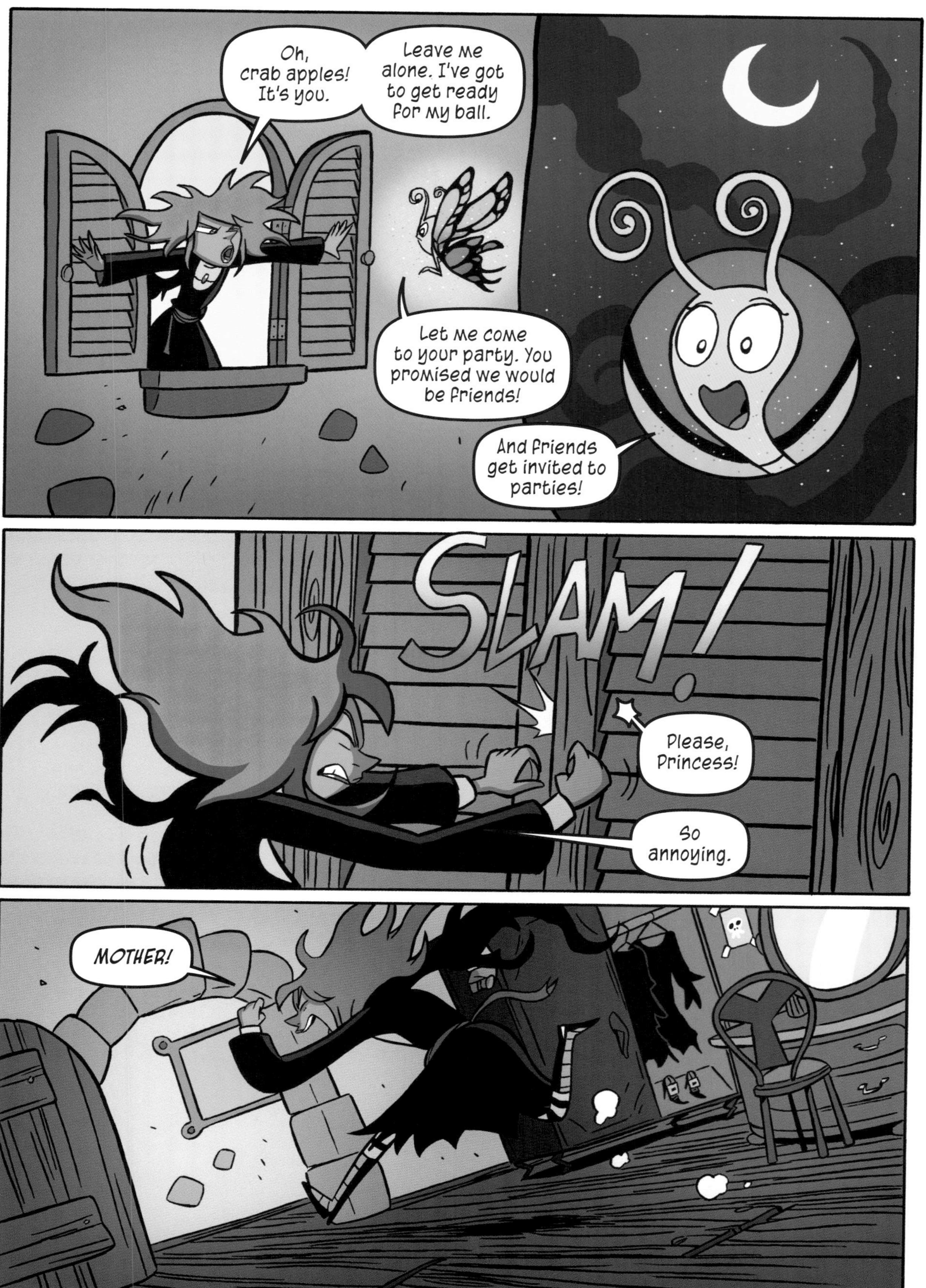

Oh, crab apples! It's you.
Leave me alone. I've got to get ready for my ball.
Let me come to your party. You promised we would be friends!
And friends get invited to parties!
SLAM!
Please, Princess!
So annoying.
MOTHER!

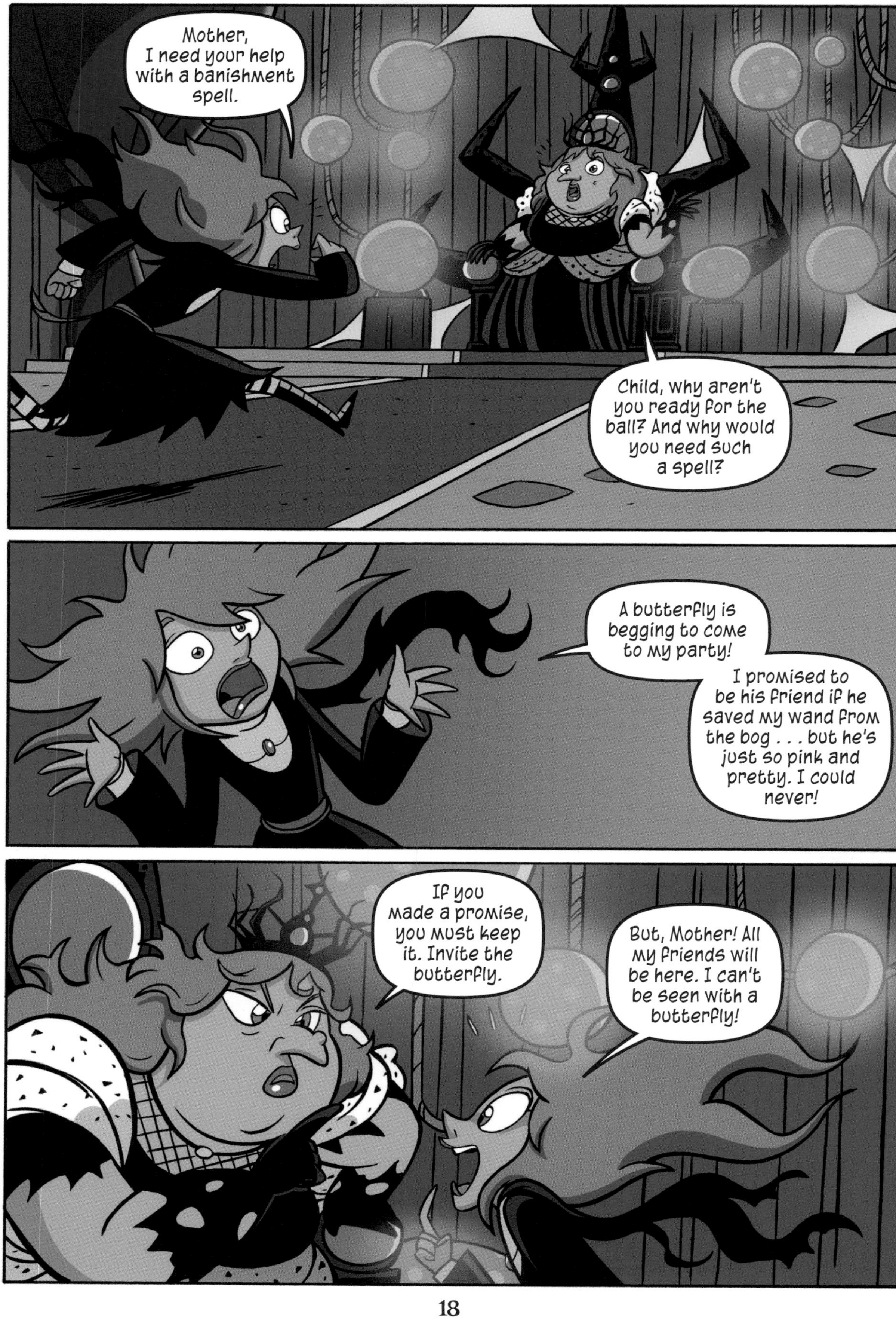
Mother, I need your help with a banishment spell.
Child, why aren't you ready for the ball? And why would you need such a spell?
A butterfly is begging to come to my party!
I promised to be his friend if he saved my wand from the bog . . . but he's just so pink and pretty. I could never!
If you made a promise, you must keep it. Invite the butterfly.
But, Mother! All my friends will be here. I can't be seen with a butterfly!

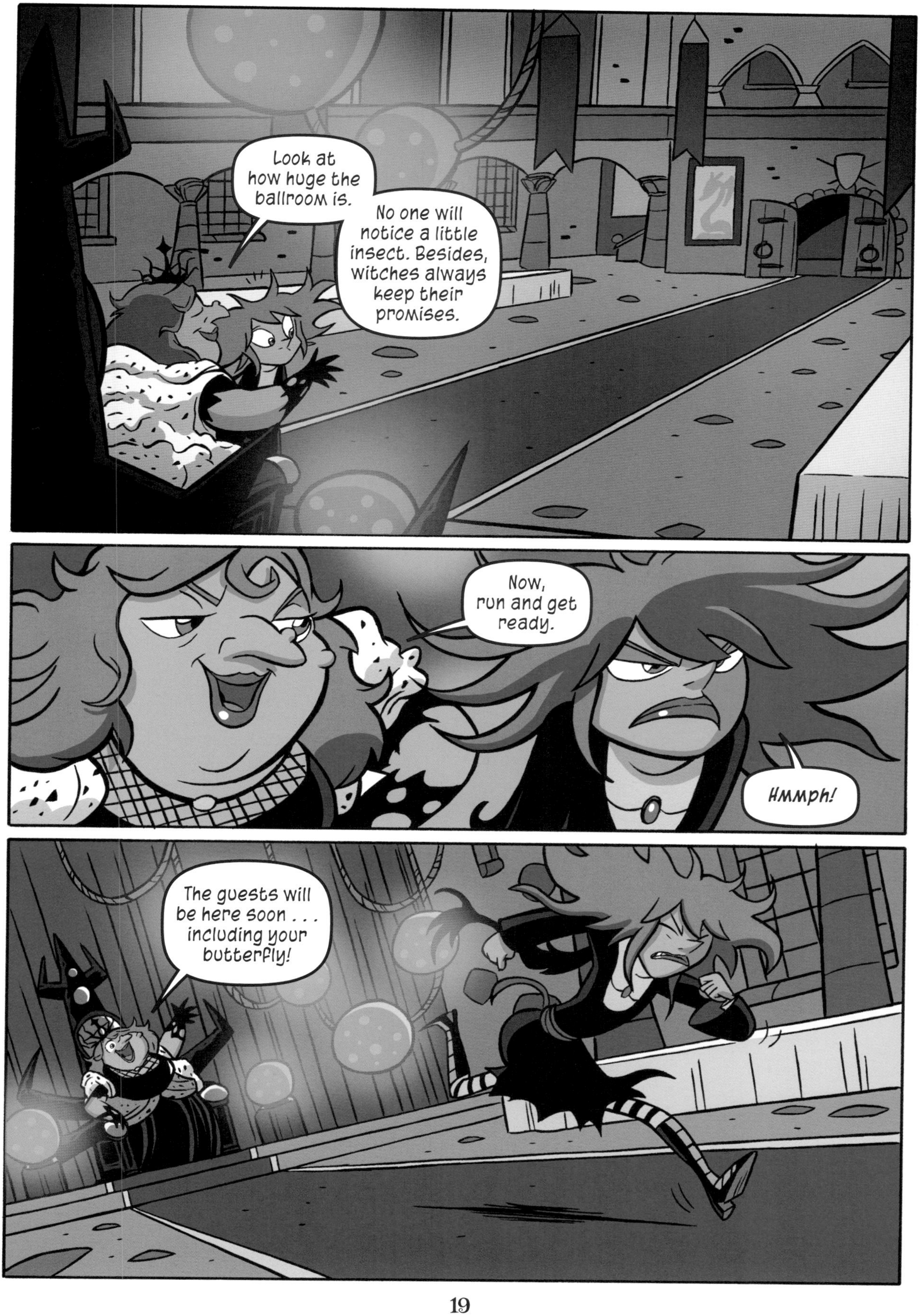
Look at how huge the ballroom is.
No one will notice a little insect. Besides, witches always keep their promises.
Now, run and get ready.
Hmmph!
The guests will be here soon . . . including your butterfly!

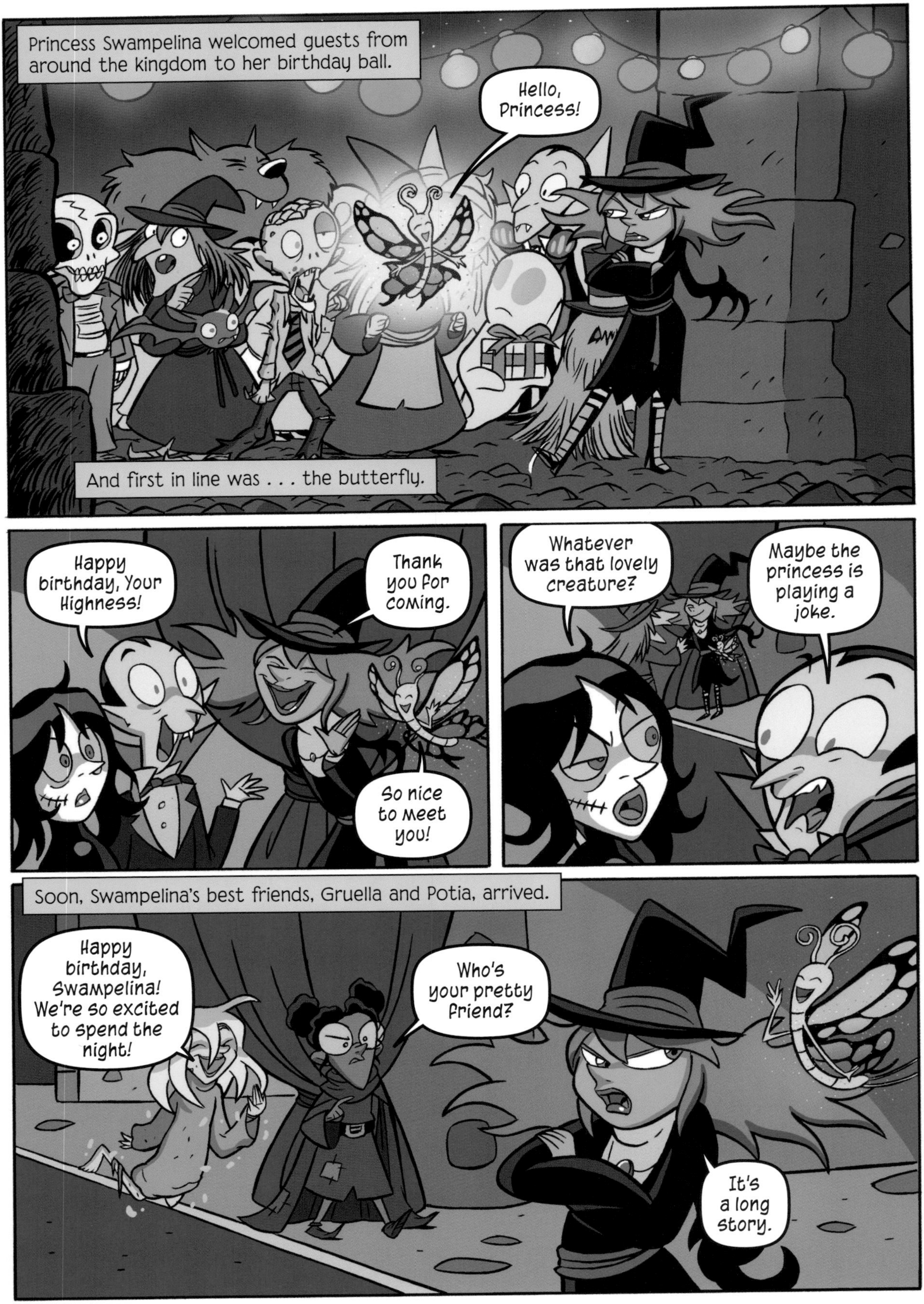

Princess Swampelina welcomed guests from around the kingdom to her birthday ball.
Hello, Princess!
And first in line was . . . the butterfly.
Happy birthday, Your Highness!
Thank you for coming.
So nice to meet you!
Whatever was that lovely creature?
Maybe the princess is playing a joke.
Soon, Swampelina's best friends, Gruella and Potia, arrived.
Happy birthday, Swampelina! We're so excited to spend the night!
Who's your pretty friend?
It's a long story.

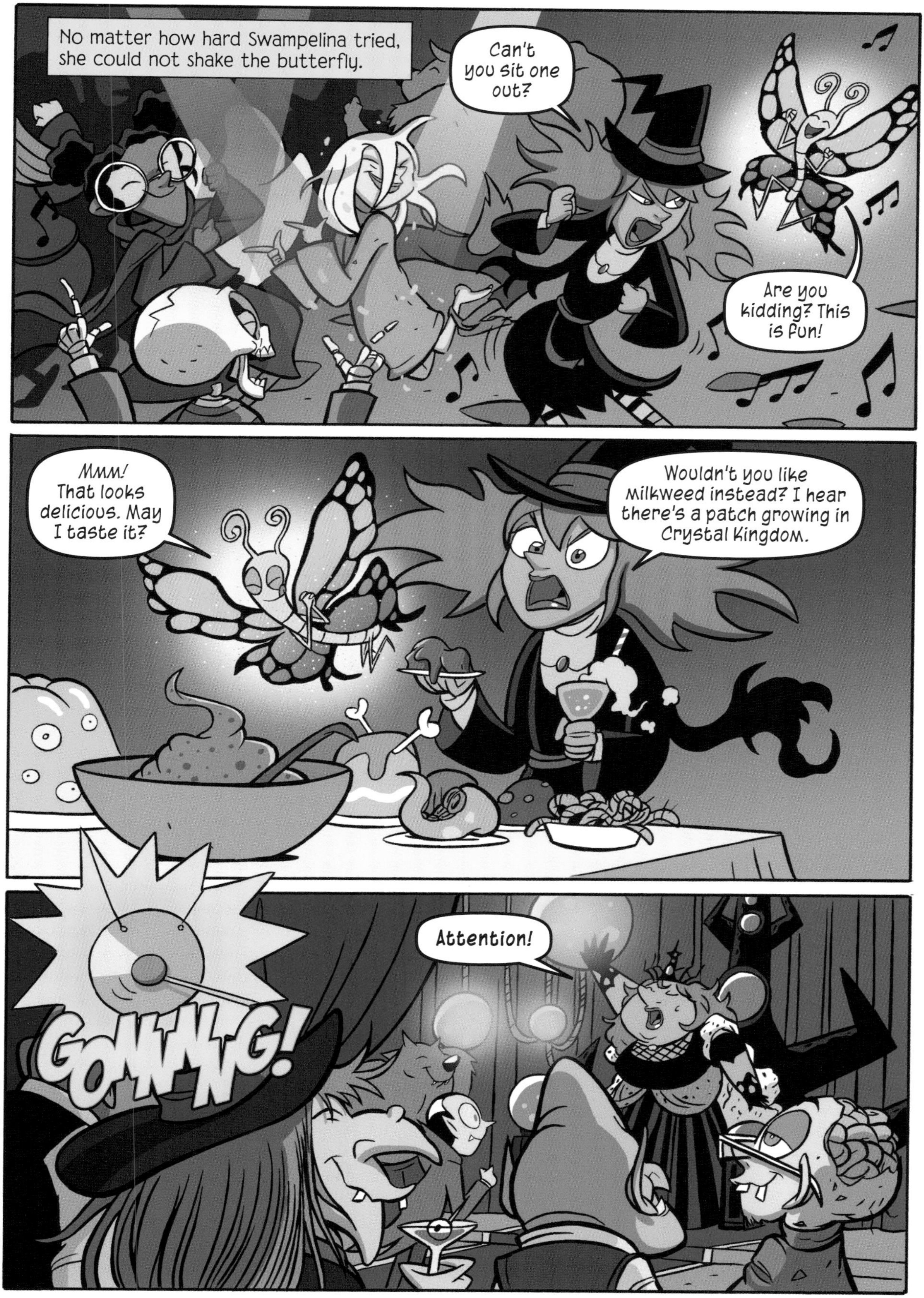
No matter how hard Swampelina tried, she could not shake the butterfly.
Can't you sit one out?
Are you kidding? This is fun!
Mmm! That looks delicious. May I taste it?
Wouldn't you like milkweed instead? I hear there's a patch growing in Crystal Kingdom.
GONNNG!
Attention!

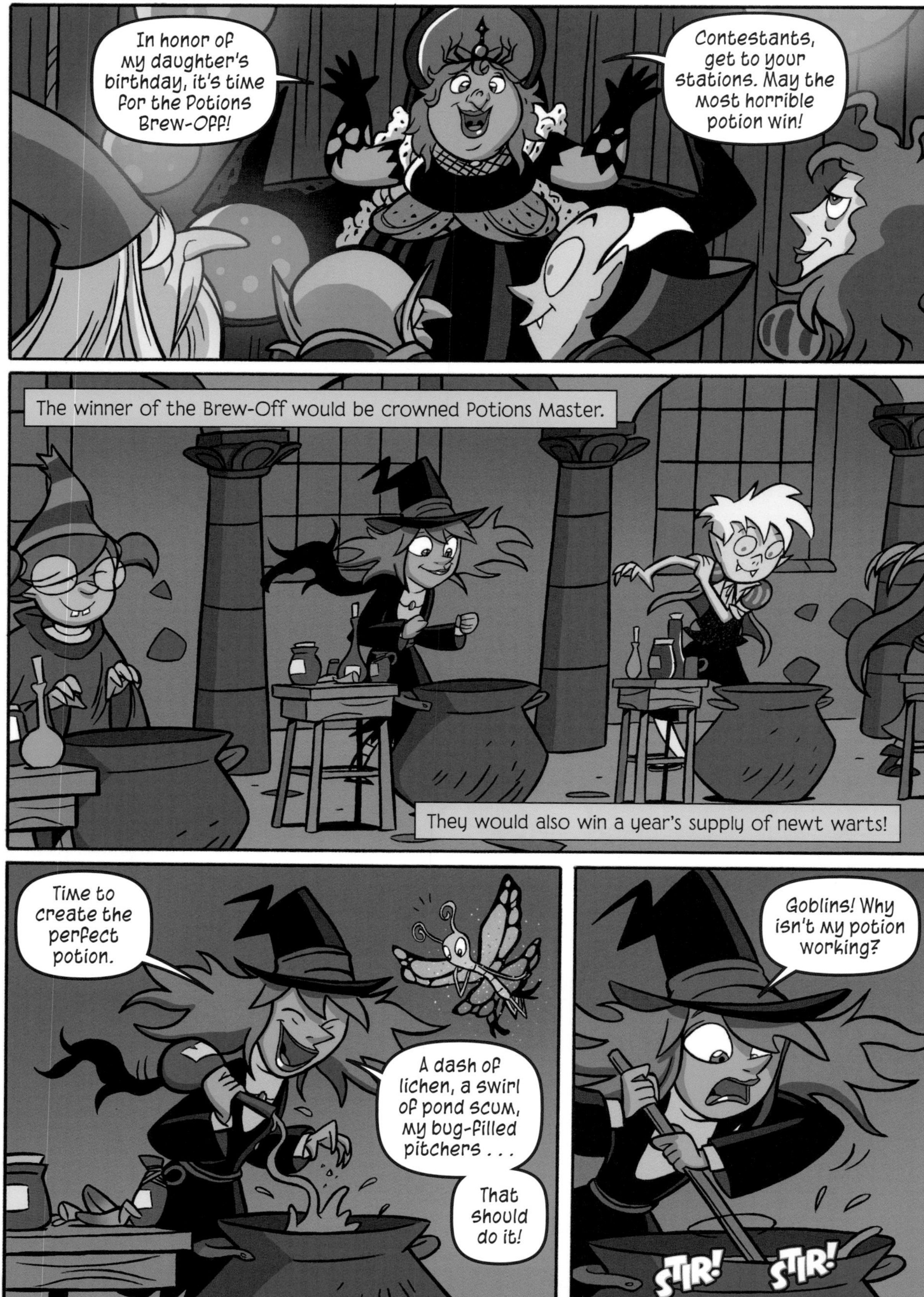
In honor of my daughter's birthday, it's time for the Potions Brew-Off!
Contestants, get to your stations. May the most horrible potion win!
The winner of the Brew-Off would be crowned Potions Master.
They would also win a year's supply of newt warts!
Time to create the perfect potion.
A dash of lichen, a swirl of pond scum, my bug-filled pitchers . . .
That should do it!
Goblins! Why isn't my potion working?
STIR! STIR!

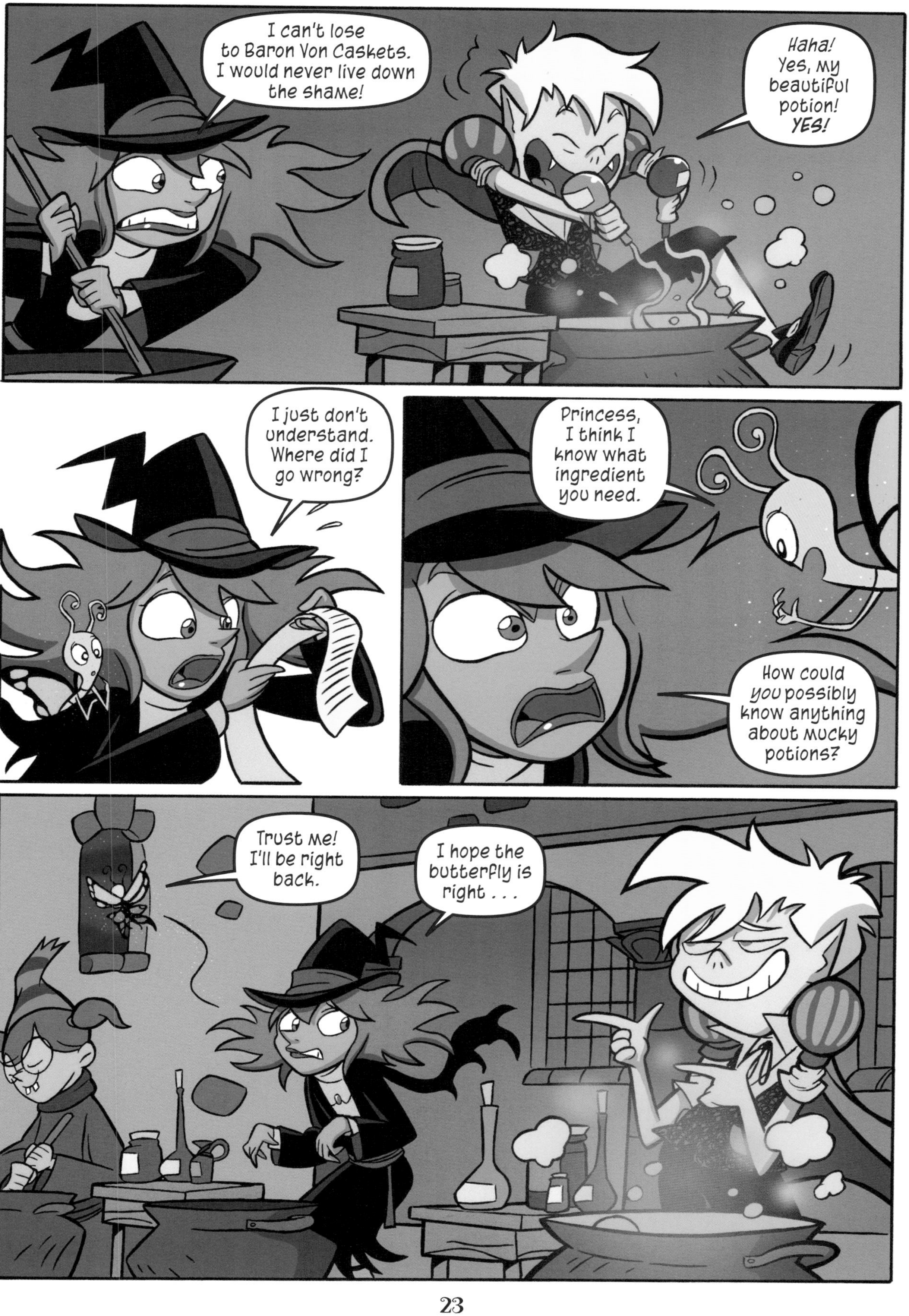
I can't lose to Baron Von Caskets. I would never live down the shame!
Haha! Yes, my beautiful potion! YES!
I just don't understand. Where did I go wrong?
Princess, I think I know what ingredient you need.
How could you possibly know anything about mucky potions?
Trust me! I'll be right back.
I hope the butterfly is right . . .

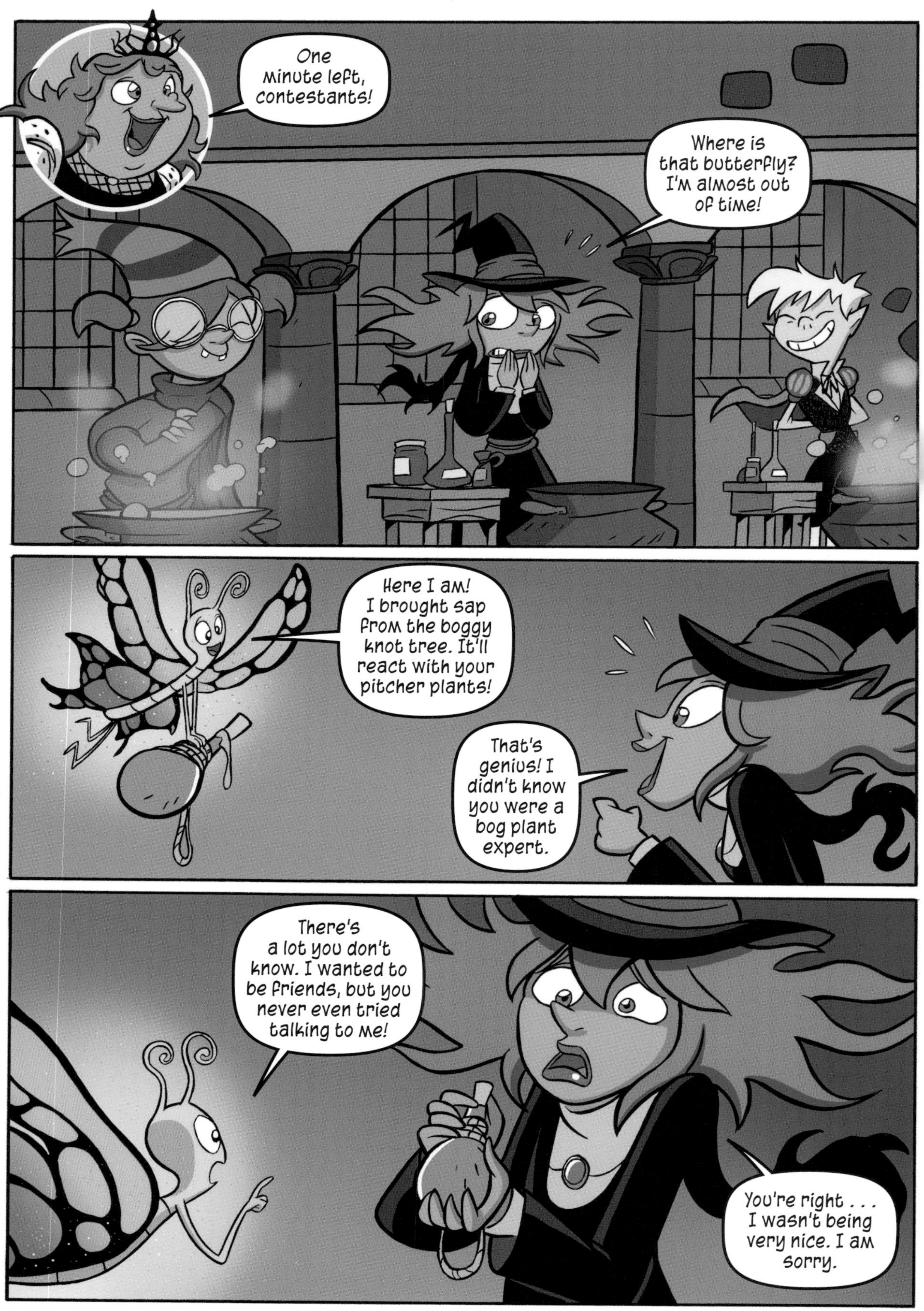
One minute left, contestants!
Where is that butterfly? I'm almost out of time!
Here I am! I brought sap from the boggy knot tree. It'll react with your pitcher plants!
That's genius! I didn't know you were a bog plant expert.
There's a lot you don't know. I wanted to be friends, but you never even tried talking to me!
You're right . . . I wasn't being very nice. I am sorry.

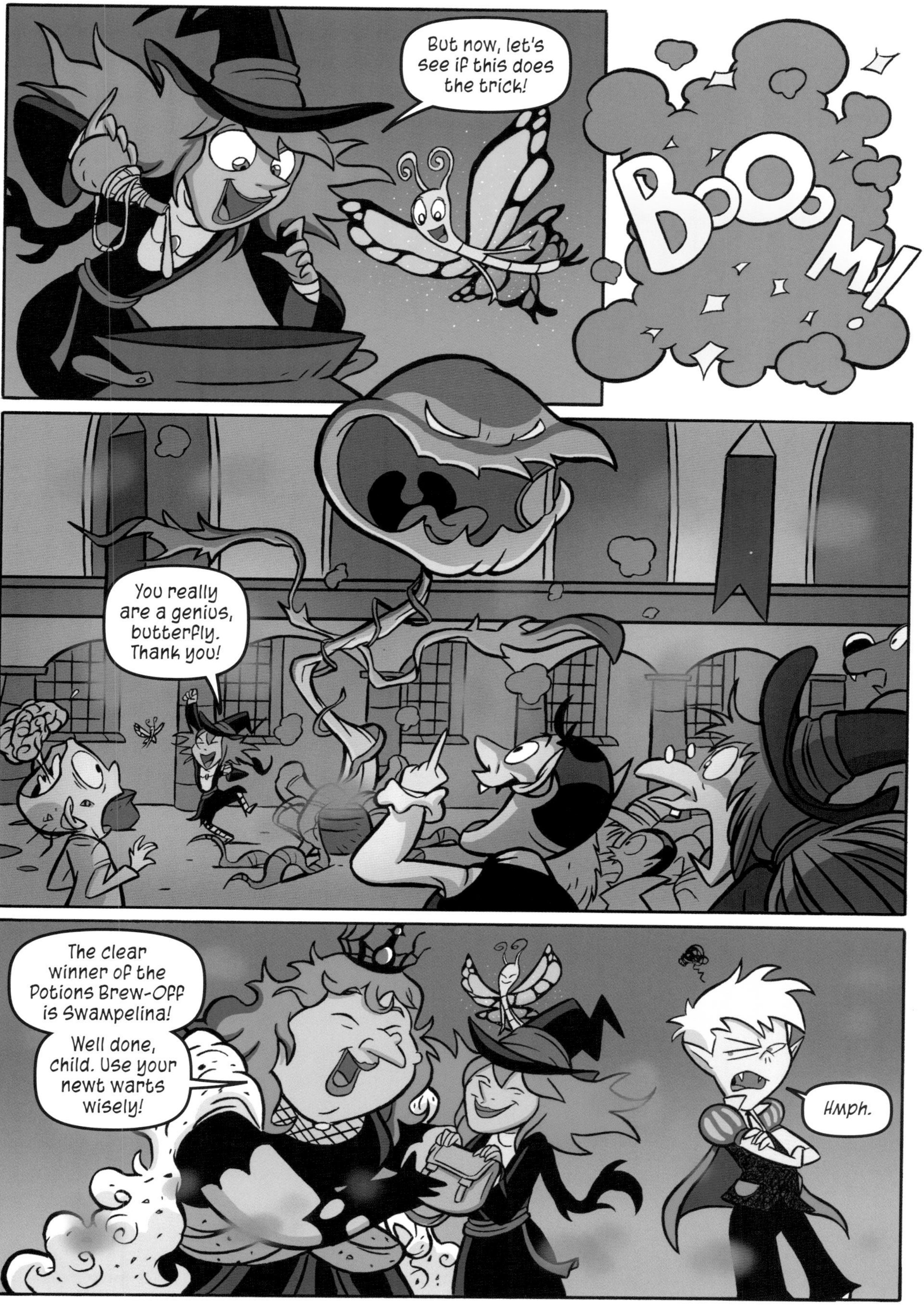
But now, let's see if this does the trick!
BOOOM!
You really are a genius, butterfly. Thank you!
The clear winner of the Potions Brew-Off is Swampelina!
Well done, child. Use your newt warts wisely!
Hmph.

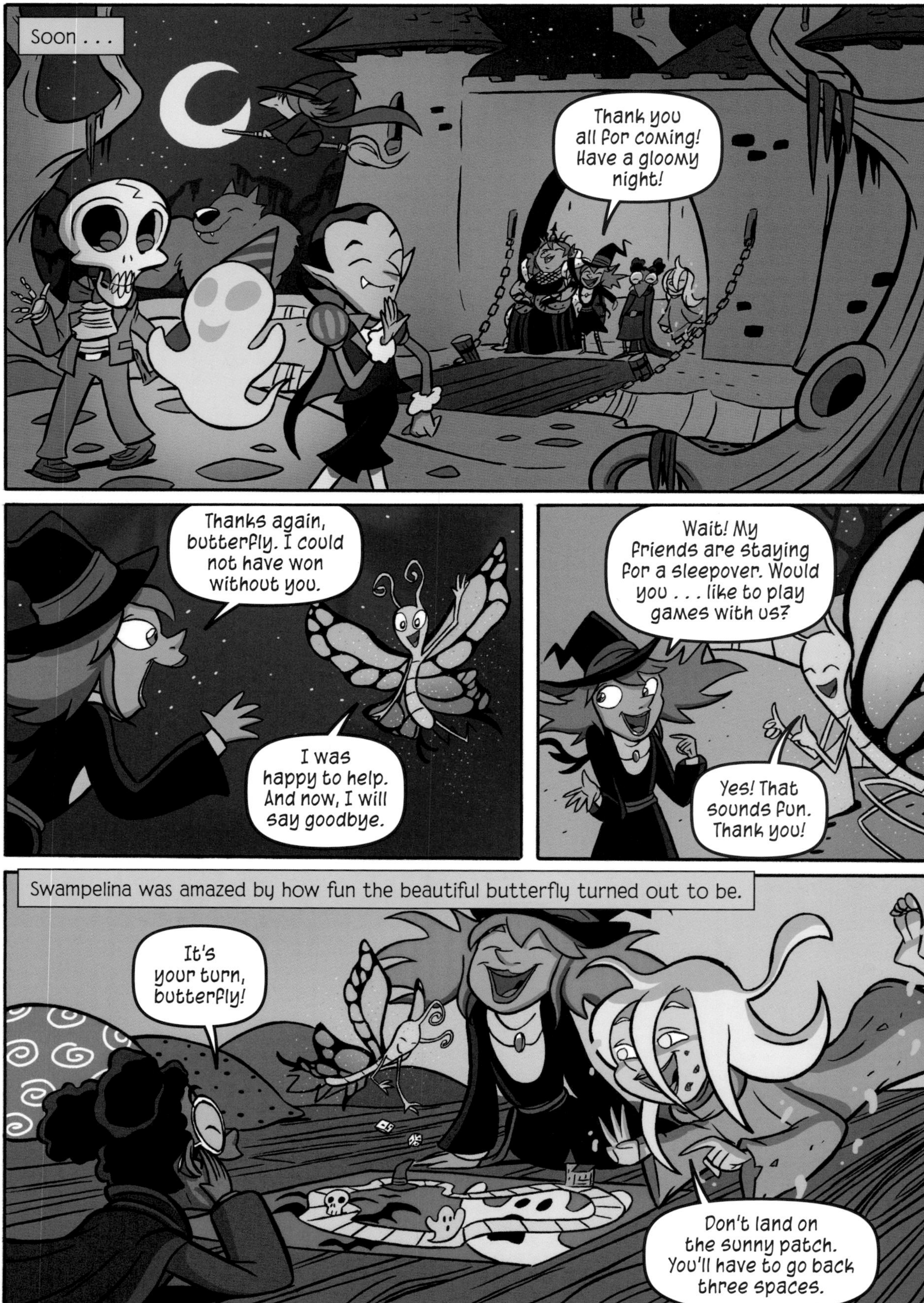
Soon . . .
Thank you all for coming! Have a gloomy night!
Thanks again, butterfly. I could not have won without you.
I was happy to help. And now, I will say goodbye.
Wait! My friends are staying for a sleepover. Would you . . . like to play games with us?
Yes! That sounds fun. Thank you!
Swampelina was amazed by how fun the beautiful butterfly turned out to be.
It's your turn, butterfly!
Don't land on the sunny patch. You'll have to go back three spaces.

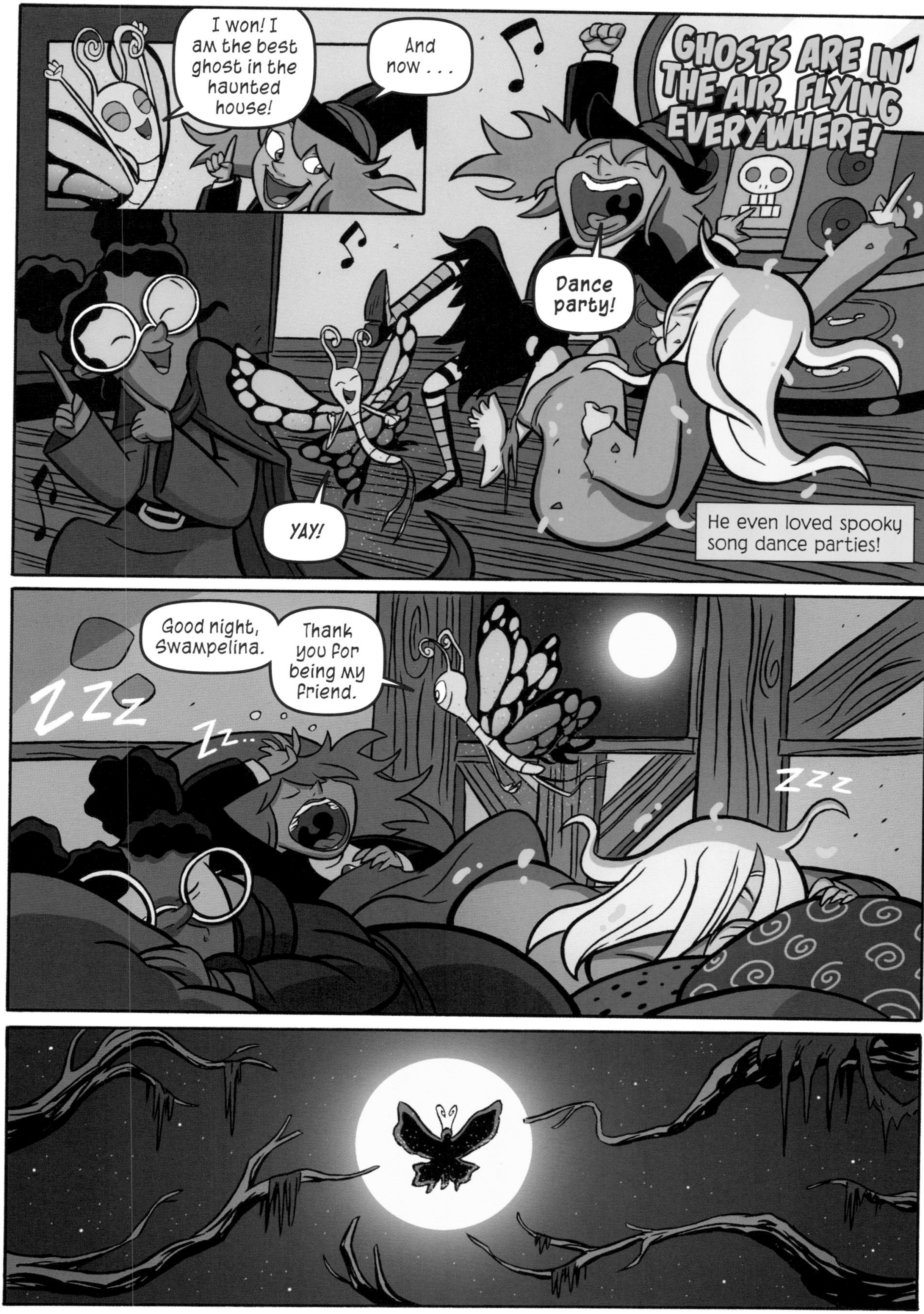
I won! I am the best ghost in the haunted house!
And now . . .
GHOSTS ARE IN THE AIR, FLYING EVERYWHERE!
Dance party!
YAY!
He even loved spooky song dance parties!
Good night, Swampelina.
Thank you for being my friend.
ZZZ
Zz..
ZZZ

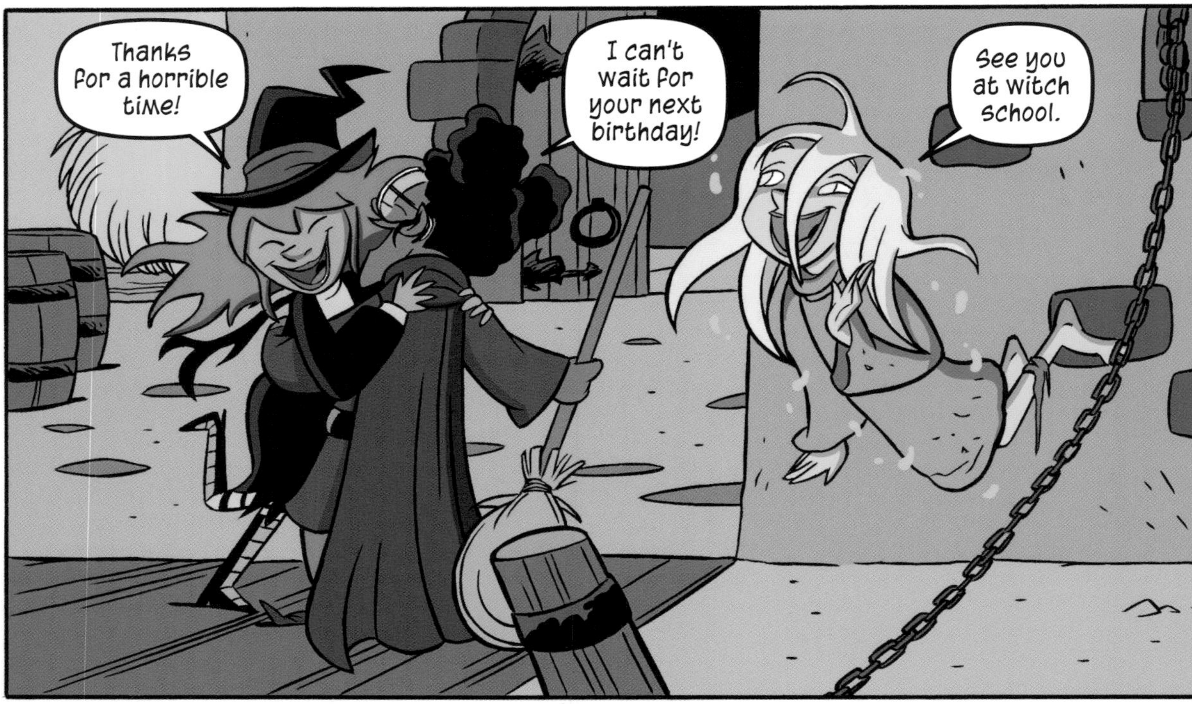
Thanks for a horrible time!
I can't wait for your next birthday!
See you at witch school.

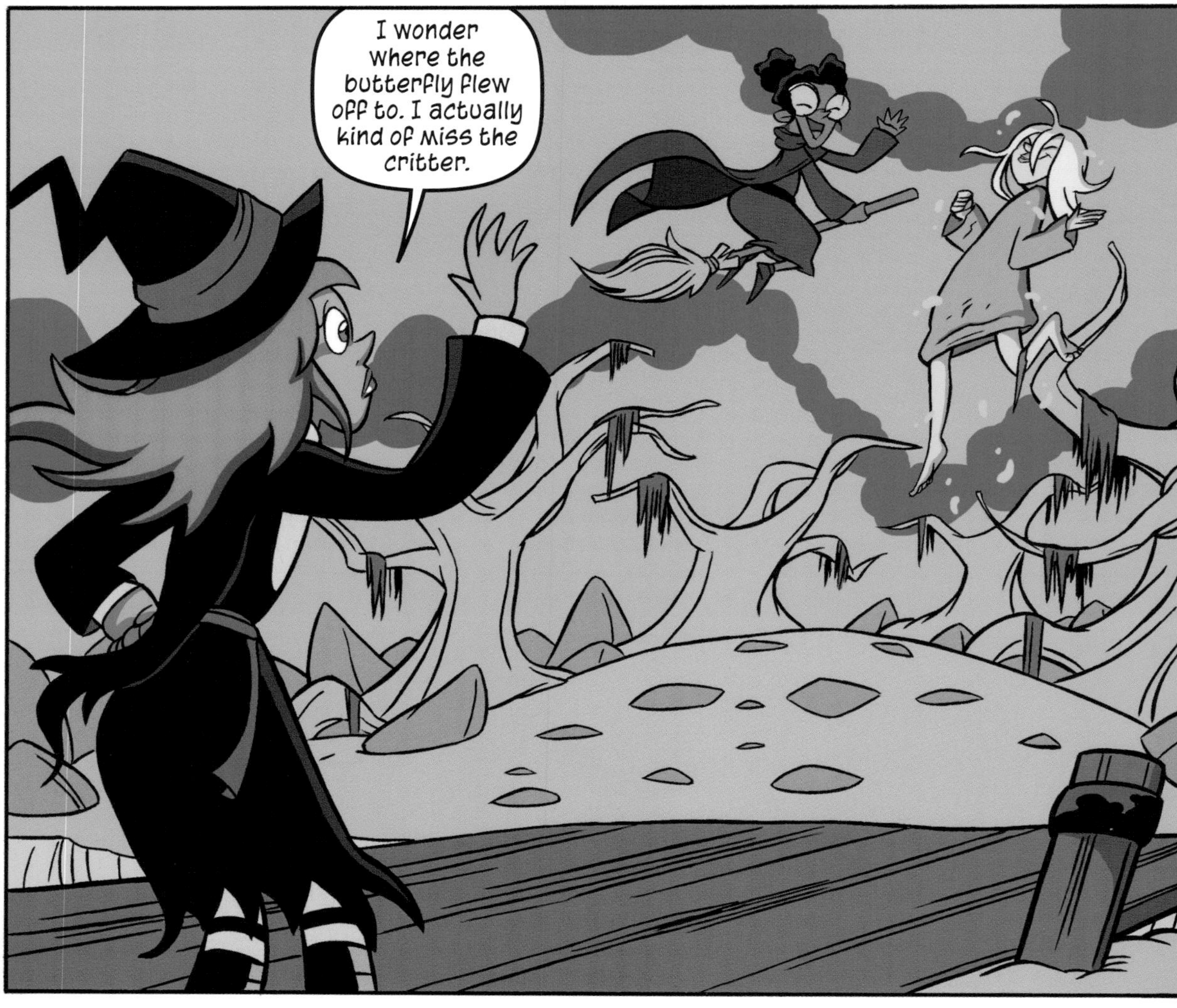
I wonder where the butterfly flew off to. I actually kind of miss the critter.

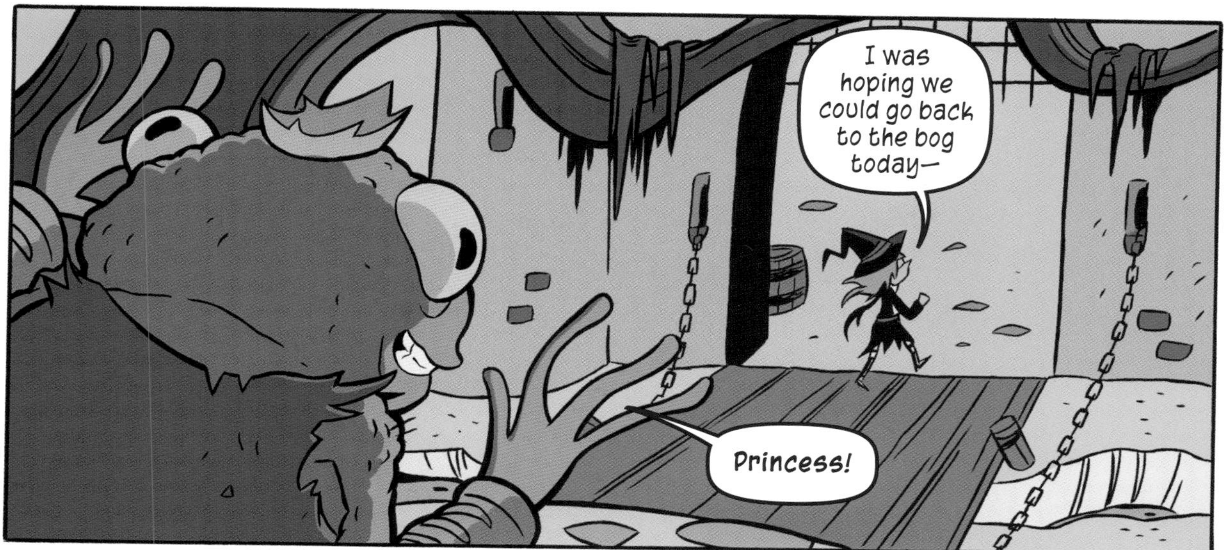
I was hoping we could go back to the bog today—
Princess!
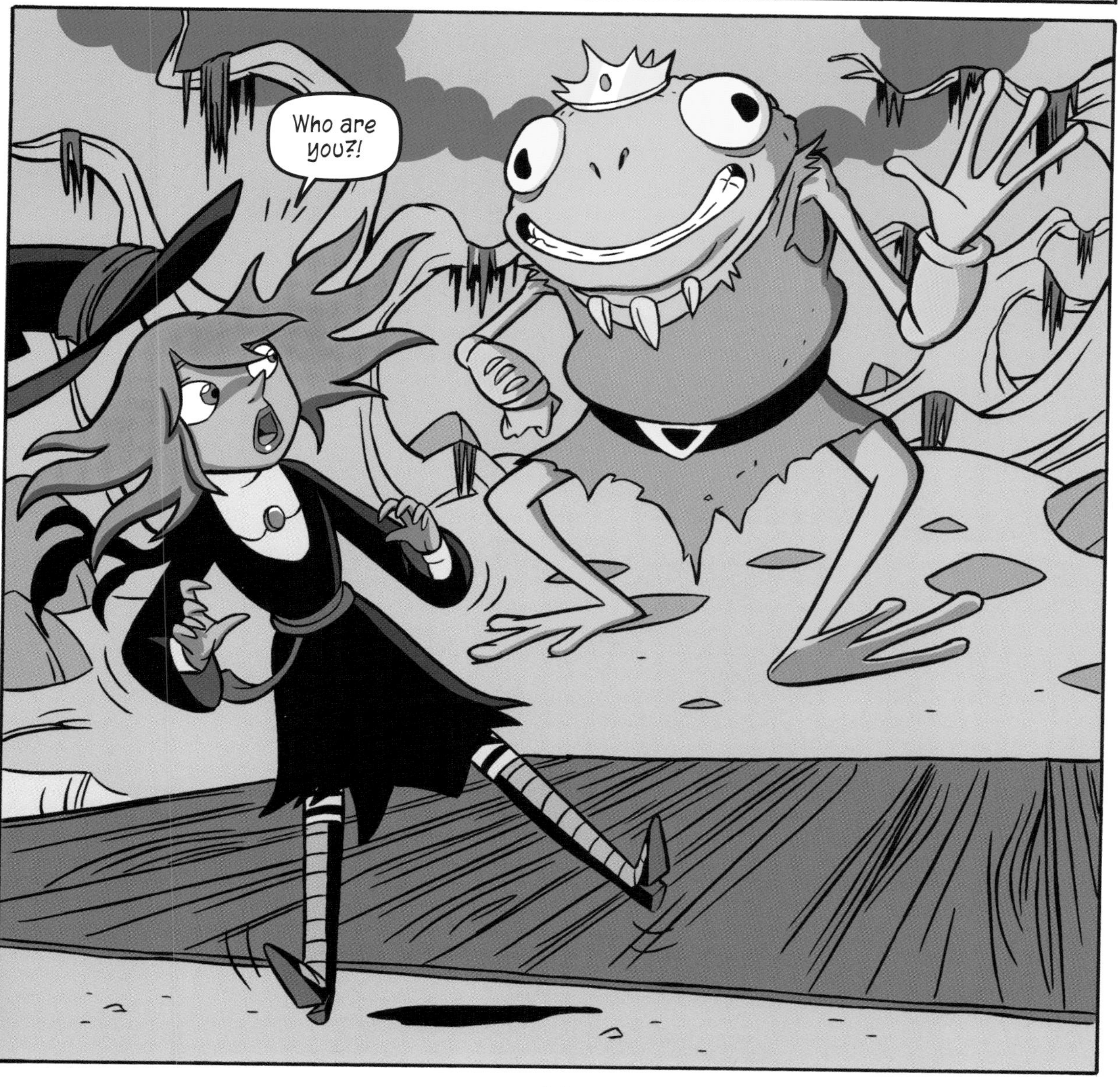
Who are you?!

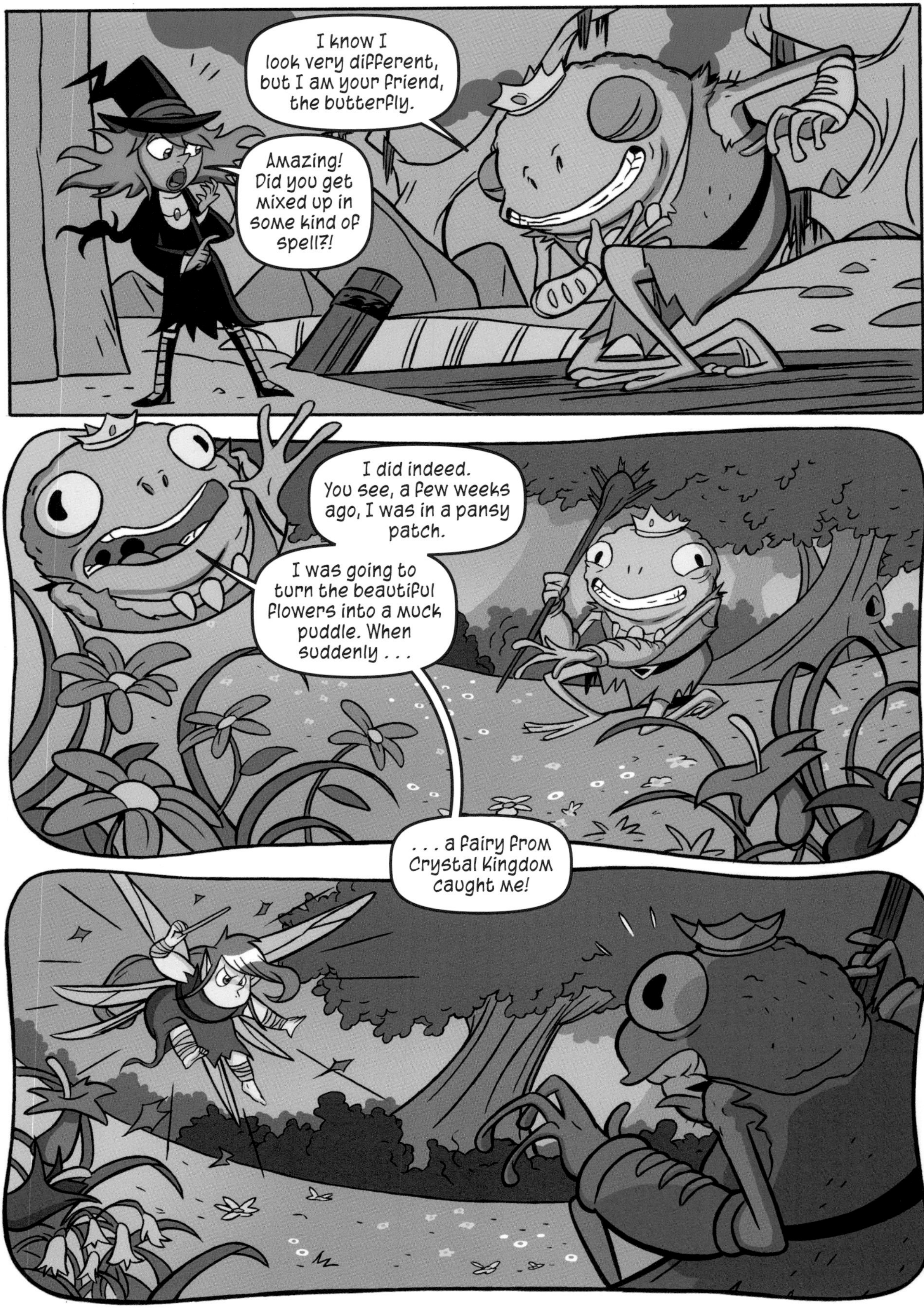
I know I look very different, but I am your friend, the butterfly.
Amazing! Did you get mixed up in some kind of spell?!
I did indeed. You see, a few weeks ago, I was in a pansy patch.
I was going to turn the beautiful flowers into a muck puddle. When suddenly . . .
. . . a fairy from Crystal Kingdom caught me!

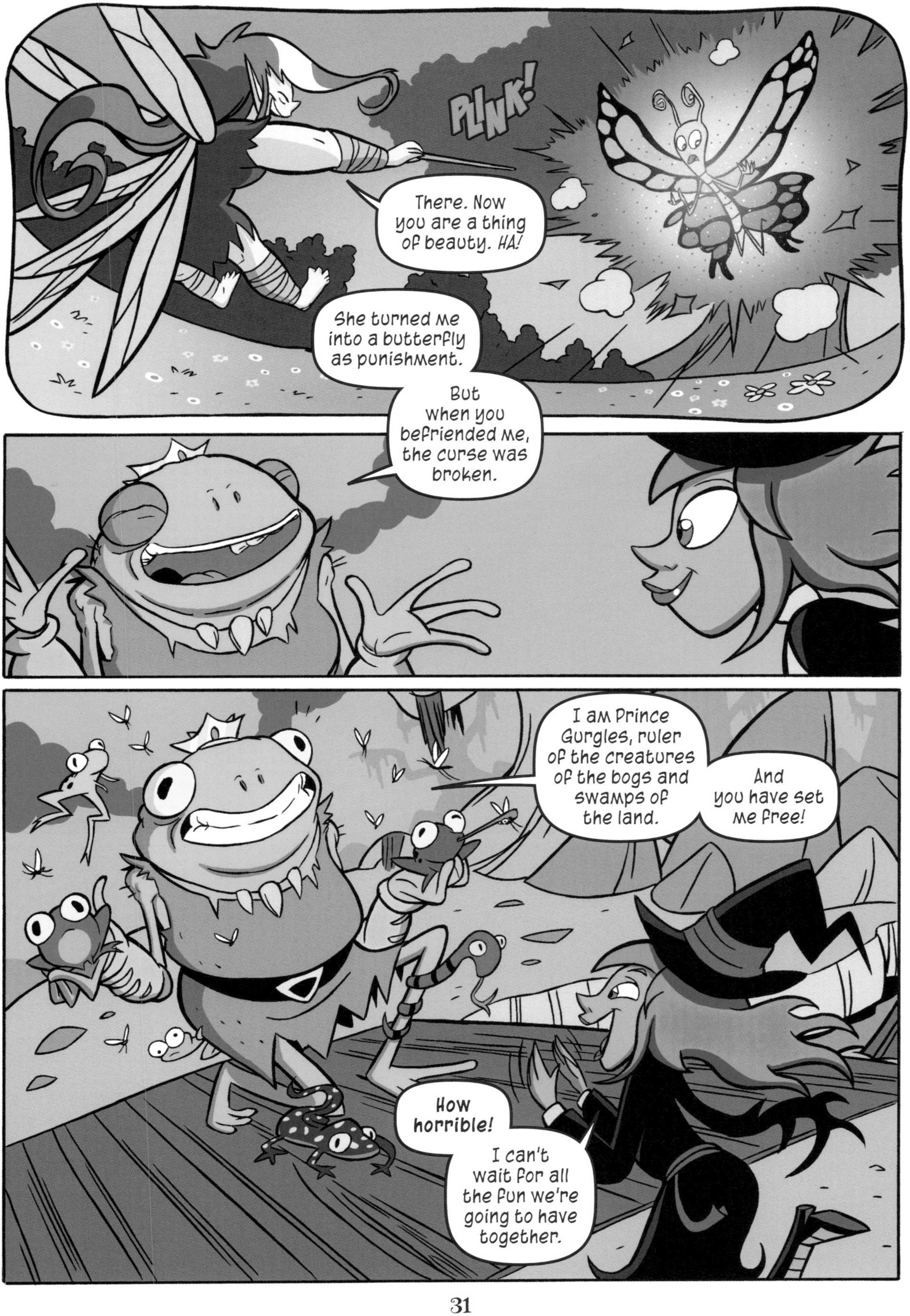
PLINK!
There. Now you are a thing of beauty. HA!
She turned me into a butterfly as punishment.
But when you befriended me, the curse was broken.
I am Prince Gurgles, ruler of the creatures of the bogs and swamps of the land.
And you have set me free!
How horrible!
I can't wait for all the fun we're going to have together.

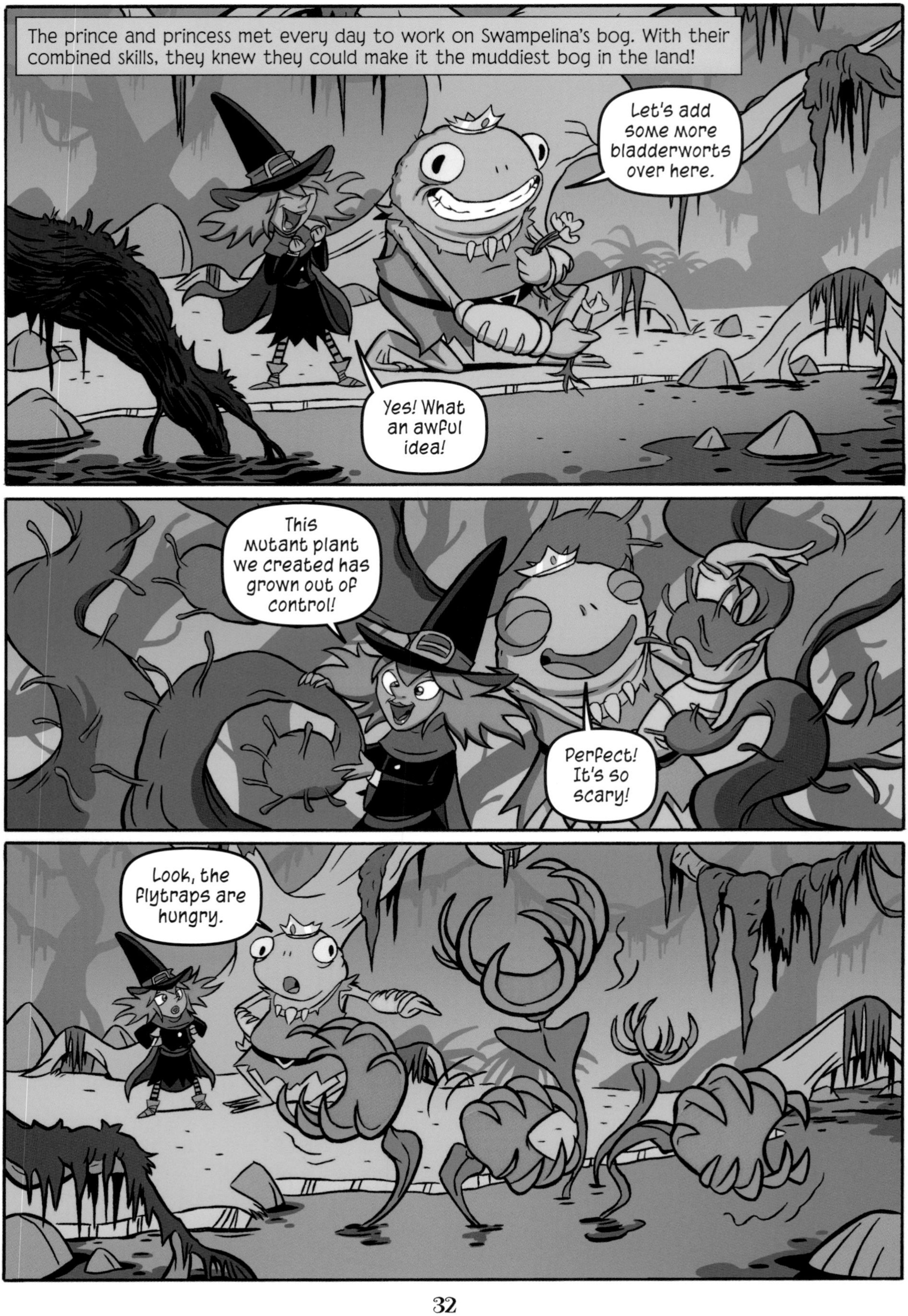

The prince and princess met every day to work on Swampelina's bog. With their combined skills, they knew they could make it the muddiest bog in the land!
Let's add some more bladderworts over here.
Yes! What an awful idea!
This mutant plant we created has grown out of control!
Perfect! It's so scary!
Look, the flytraps are hungry.

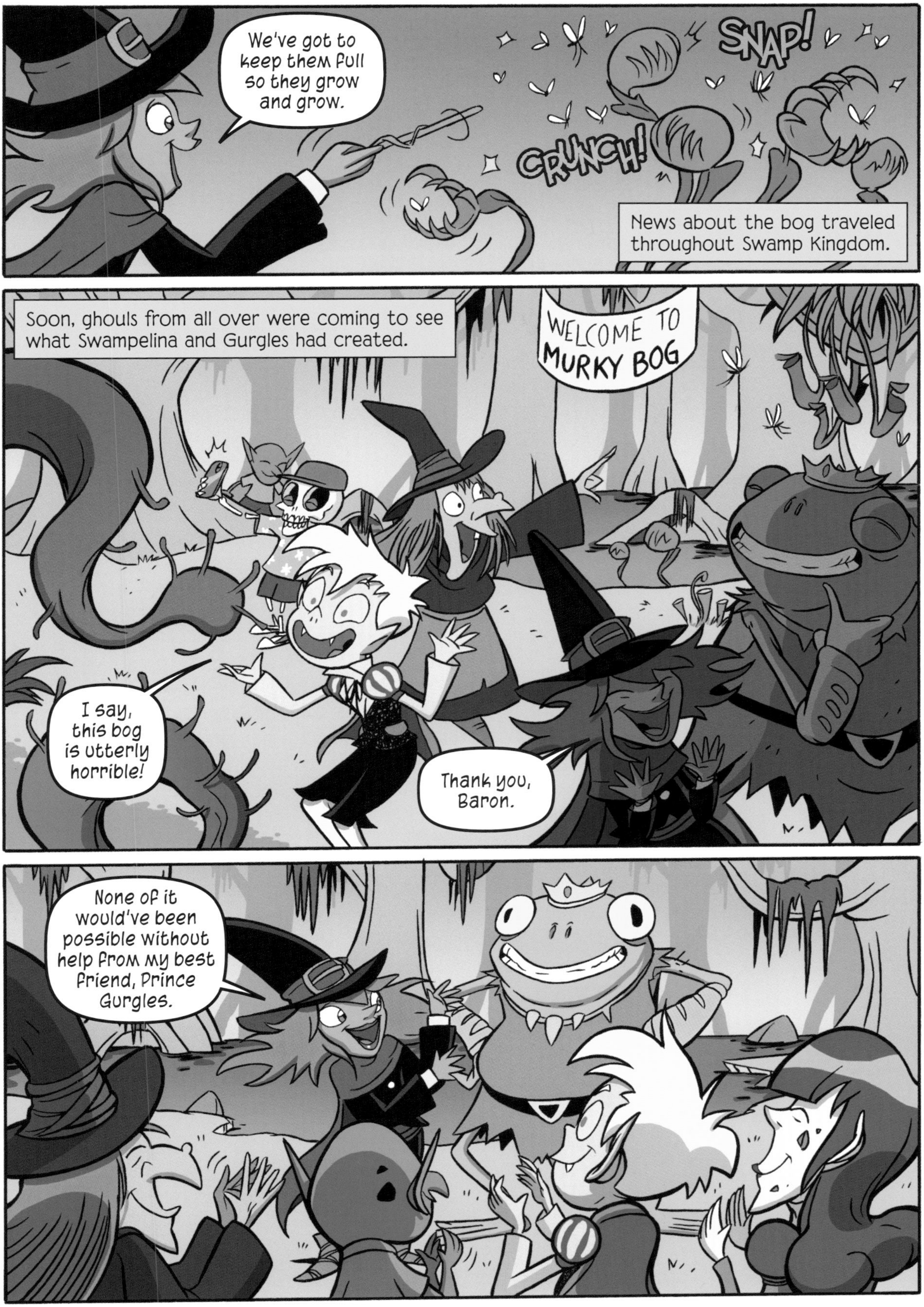
We've got to keep them full so they grow and grow.
SNAP!
CRUNCH!
News about the bog traveled throughout Swamp Kingdom.
Soon, ghouls from all over were coming to see what Swampelina and Gurgles had created.
WELCOME TO MURKY BOG
I say, this bog is utterly horrible!
Thank you, Baron.
None of it would've been possible without help from my best friend, Prince Gurgles.

ALL ABOUT THE ORIGINAL TALE!

"The Frog Prince" was first published in 1812 by the Brothers Grimm. It's the first story in a collection of folktales. Like the far out version, the original story featured a frog. But the princess was not at all happy to meet an amphibian!

In the story, a princess is playing with a golden ball when she accidentally bounces it into a well. She starts to cry, and suddenly a frog pops out of the water to ask what's the matter. He offers to retrieve the lost ball, if the princess promises to be his friend. The princess agrees. But really, she's grossed out and doesn't want to be seen with the creature! As soon as the frog brings back the ball, she runs away.

The princess forgets all about the frog. But soon he appears at the castle, asking to be let in. When the princess complains about her unwelcome visitor, the king says she must keep her promise. She must be the frog's friend. So, the princess opens the castle door and lets the frog in. The frog sticks by the princess the whole day. He eats from her plate and later sleeps on her pillow.

But the frog is no ordinary animal. He's actually a handsome prince who was cursed by an evil fairy! In the original story, the princess's friendship breaks the spell. In some versions of the tale, the princess's kiss does it. But in one version, the princess wants the frog to go away so badly that she takes extreme action. She throws the frog against a wall! Luckily, that actually breaks the curse, and the frog turns back into a prince. In all the stories, the prince and princess go on to marry, and they live happily ever after.

A FAR OUT GUIDE TO THE TALE'S WITCHY TWISTS!

The original princess is grossed out by the frog. But witch Swampelina loves all things yucky and doesn't like the pretty butterfly!

The far out princess accidentally loses her precious magic wand, not a golden ball.

 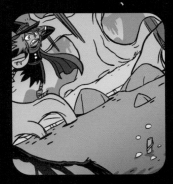

In the original, the princess must let the frog eat dinner with her. In this version, Swampelina must invite the butterfly to her spooky birthday ball.

The Grimm tale ends with marriage, but Swampelina doesn't marry someone she just met. Instead, she and Gurgles become best friends!

VISUAL QUESTIONS

Were you surprised when Swampelina said she doesn't like pretty things? Why or why not? Explain your answer with examples from the art and text.

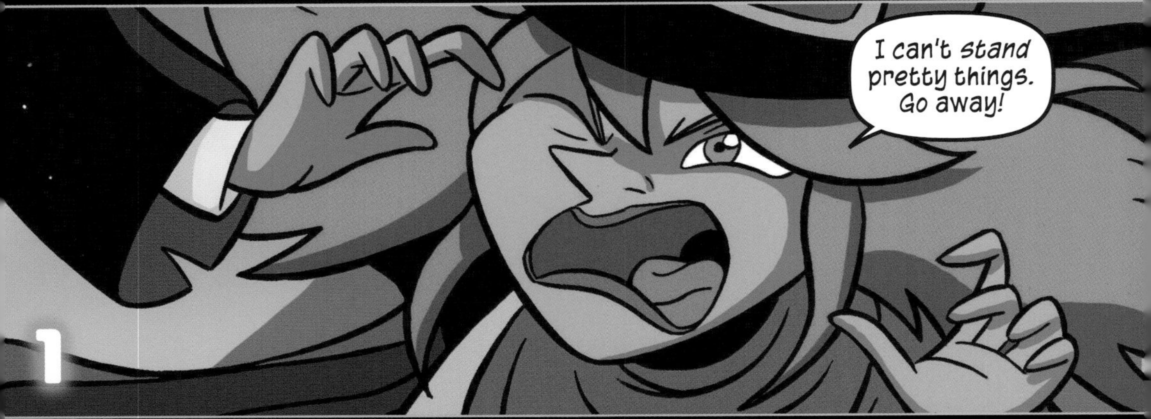
I can't stand pretty things. Go away!
1

Look closely at all of the characters' expressions in this panel from page 20. What might they be thinking? Write out thought balloons for each creature.

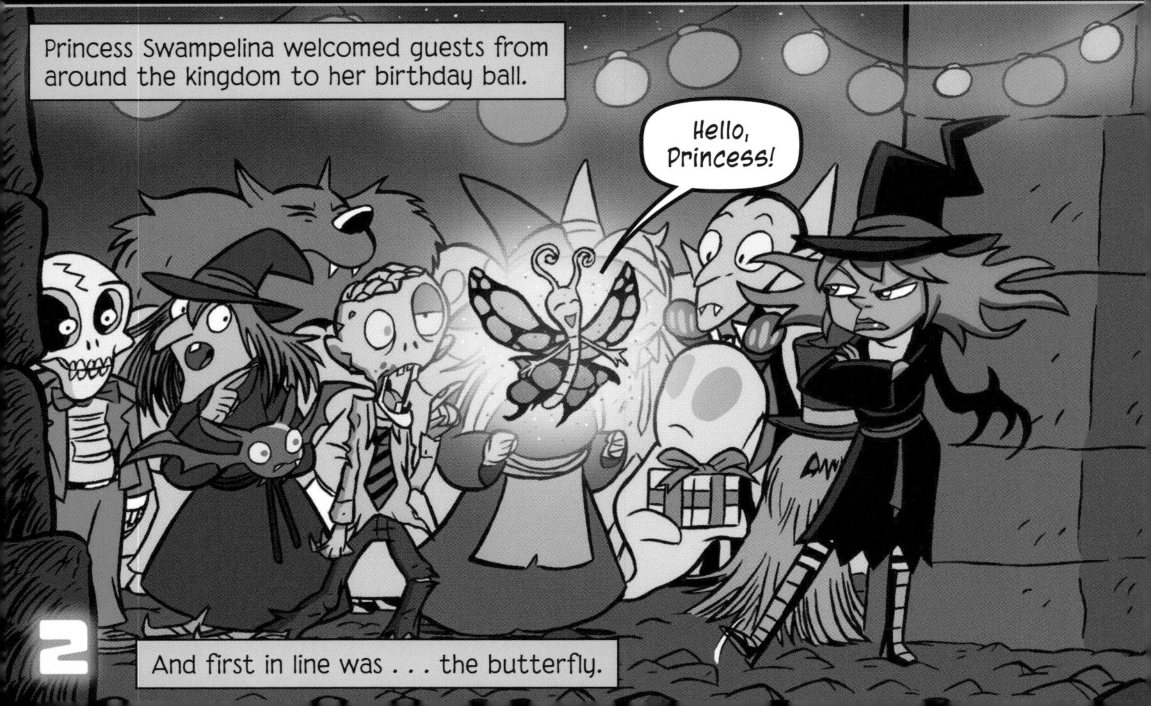
Princess Swampelina welcomed guests from around the kingdom to her birthday ball.
Hello, Princess!
2
And first in line was . . . the butterfly.

Swampelina apologizes to the butterfly. Do you think she means it? Use examples from the story to support your answer.

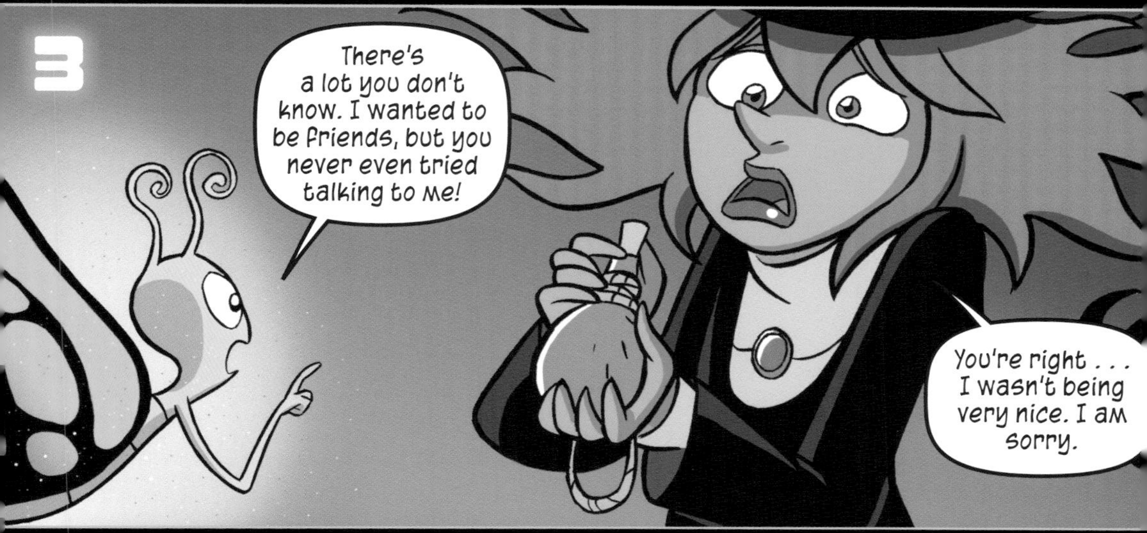
3
There's a lot you don't know. I wanted to be friends, but you never even tried talking to me!
You're right . . . I wasn't being very nice. I am sorry.

Can you list at least two ways Swampelina tries to avoid the butterfly? Flip back through the book if you need help.

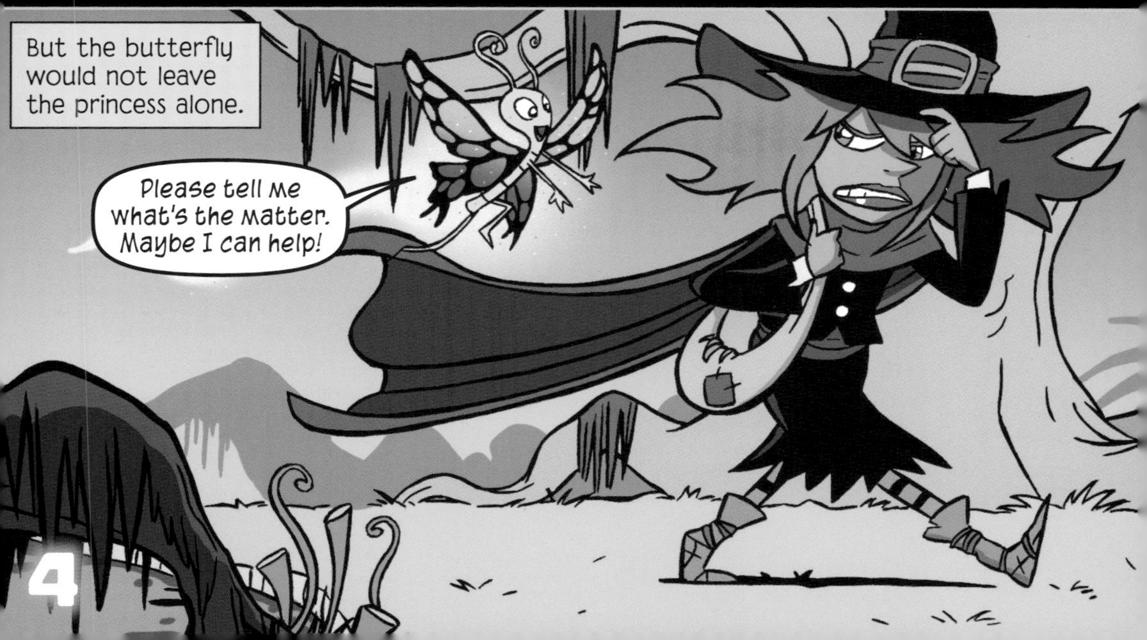
But the butterfly would not leave the princess alone.
Please tell me what's the matter. Maybe I can help!
4

AUTHOR

Benjamin Harper lives in Los Angeles where he edits superhero books for a living. When he's not at work, he writes; watches monster movies; and hangs out with his cats, Marjorie and Jerry, a betta fish named Toby, and tanks full of rough-skinned and eastern newts. He tends a garden full of carnivorous plants and also grows milkweed to help save monarch butterflies. His other books include the Bug Girl series, *Obsessed with Star Wars*, *DC Super Friends Going Bananas!*, *Hansel & Gretel & Zombies*, and many more.

ILLUSTRATOR

Álex López is from Sabadell, Spain. He became a professional illustrator and comic book artist in 2001, but he has been drawing ever since he can remember. López's pieces have been published in many countries, including the United States, United Kingdom, Spain, France, Italy, Belgium, and Turkey. He's also worked on a variety of projects, from illustrated books to video games to marketing pieces . . . but what he loves most is making comic books.

GLOSSARY

banishment (BA-nish-muhnt)—the act of forcing someone to go away, often for a long period of time

befriend (bih-FREND)—to become friends with someone

bog (BOG)—an area with wet, soft ground and pools of muddy water

carnivorous (kahr-NIH-vuh-ruhss)—eating meat; carnivorous plants trap and eat insects

condition (kuhn-DISH-uhn)—something that is promised before another thing can happen

contestant (kuhn-TES-tuhnt)—someone who's taking part in a contest

curse (KUHRS)—a spell that causes trouble or bad luck for someone

expert (EK-spurt)—a person with a lot of knowledge in something

ghastly (GAST-lee)—shocking and terrible (which, if you're Swampelina, is great!)

ghoul (GOOL)—a scary person or creature

ingredient (in-GREE-dee-uhnt)—a thing that is added to a mix in order to make something new

potion (POH-shuhn)—a liquid mixture that has magical effects

AWESOMELY EVER AFTER.

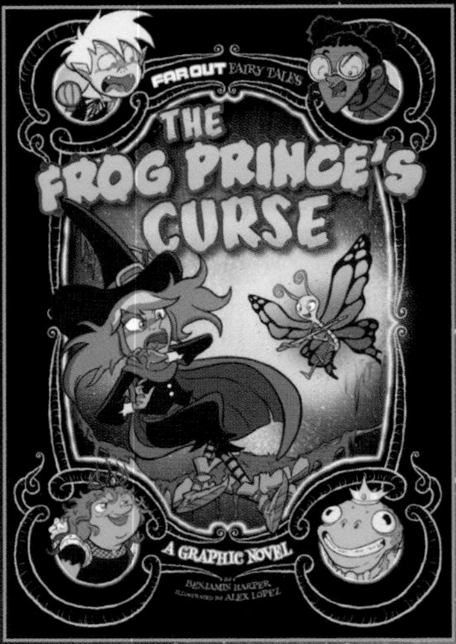
FAR OUT FAIRY TALES
THE FROG PRINCE'S CURSE
A GRAPHIC NOVEL
BY BENJAMIN HARPER
ILLUSTRATED BY ALEX LOPEZ

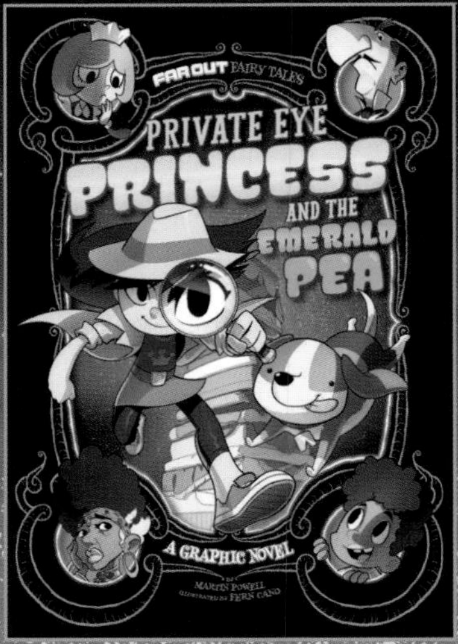
FAR OUT FAIRY TALES
PRIVATE EYE PRINCESS AND THE EMERALD PEA
A GRAPHIC NOVEL
BY MARTY POWELL
ILLUSTRATED BY FERN CANO

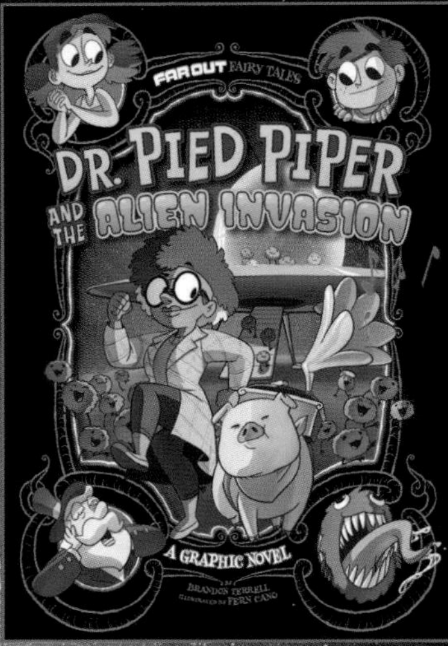
FAR OUT FAIRY TALES
DR. PIED PIPER AND THE ALIEN INVASION
A GRAPHIC NOVEL
BY BRANDON TERRELL
ILLUSTRATED BY FERN CANO

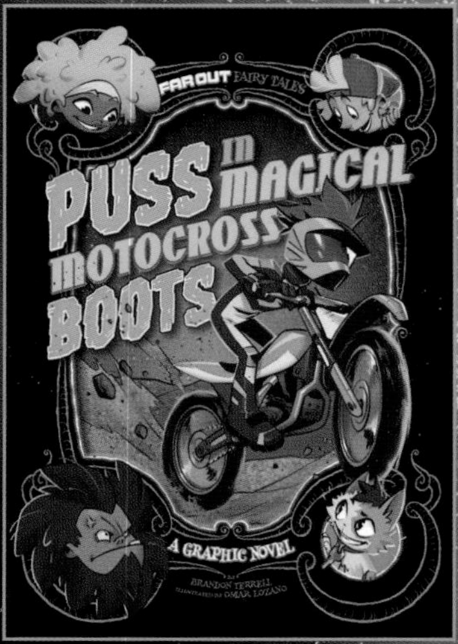
FAR OUT FAIRY TALES
PUSS IN MAGICAL MOTOCROSS BOOTS
A GRAPHIC NOVEL
BY BRANDON TERRELL
ILLUSTRATED BY OMAR LOZANO

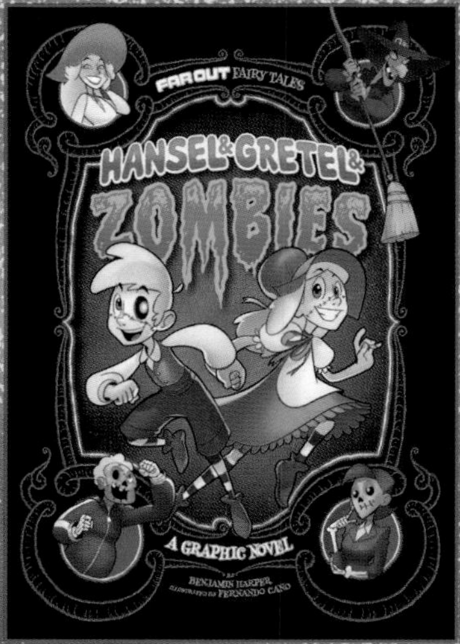
FAR OUT FAIRY TALES
HANSEL & GRETEL & ZOMBIES
A GRAPHIC NOVEL
BY BENJAMIN HARPER
ILLUSTRATED BY FERNANDO CANO

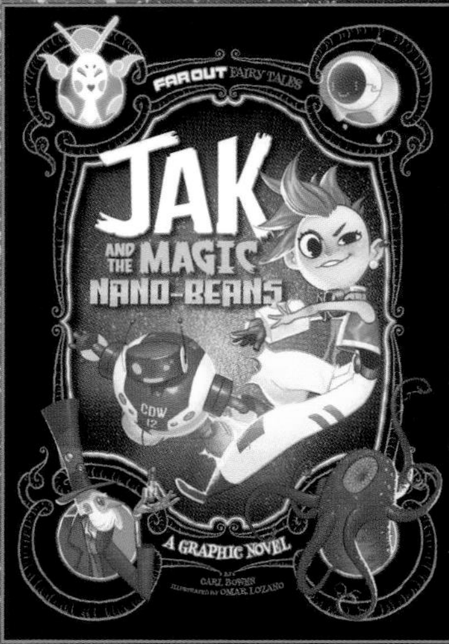
FAR OUT FAIRY TALES
JAK AND THE MAGIC NANO-BEANS
A GRAPHIC NOVEL
BY CARL BOWEN
ILLUSTRATED BY OMAR LOZANO

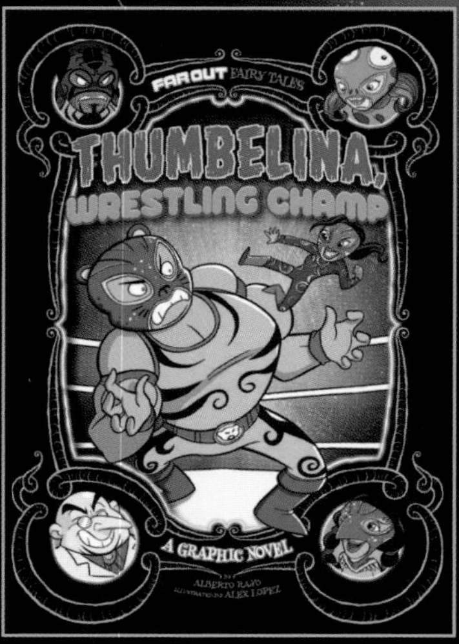
FAR OUT FAIRY TALES
THUMBELINA, WRESTLING CHAMP
A GRAPHIC NOVEL
BY ALBERTO RAYO
ILLUSTRATED BY ALEX LOPEZ

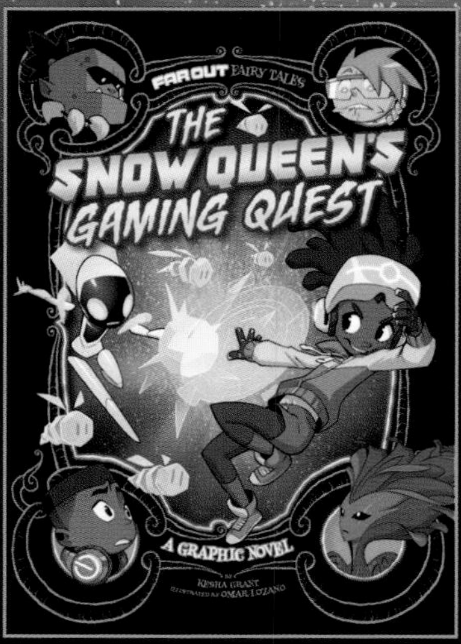
FAR OUT FAIRY TALES
THE SNOW QUEEN'S GAMING QUEST
A GRAPHIC NOVEL
BY KESHA GRANT
ILLUSTRATED BY OMAR LOZANO

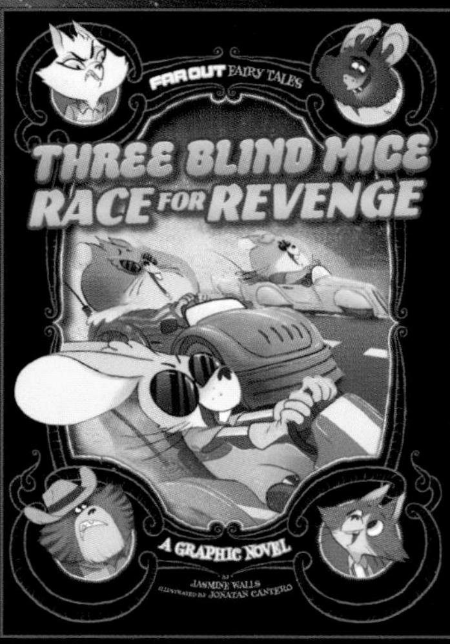
FAR OUT FAIRY TALES
THREE BLIND MICE RACE FOR REVENGE
A GRAPHIC NOVEL
BY JASMINE WALLS
ILLUSTRATED BY JONATAN CANTERO